# Never Again

Priscilla J. Krahn

# DEDICATION

To my loving and encouraging siblings, for putting up with my writing and my constant random questions that come with my writing.

છ×૪ა

"In everything give thanks: for this is the will of God in Christ Jesus concerning you." I Thessalonians 5:18

# TABLE OF CONTENTS

# ACKNOWLEDGMENTS

First of all I want to thank my Mom for all of her encouragement, advice, and help in every area. Not only did she help me edit, she did a lot of my graphic art work. I want to thank Krystal Jeffery for allowing me to use her picture on the cover. I want to thank all of my siblings for doing extra work and therefore leaving me with more time to write. I especially want to thank Hosanna Krahn and Miriam Krahn for their sacrifice of time, their opinions, and their help editing. I want to thank Grandma Sally for her amazing sacrifice of time and helping me edit. And last, but most important, I want to thank God for the lessons He has taught me through writing this book.

# CHAPTER 1
# THE SHERIFF'S NEWS

I blinked my eyes open and gazed at the fields racing by. "Where are we? And how long have I been sleeping?" I yawned, and then winced at the pain in my ribs.

Something about yawning always hurt my side. It must be the stretching motion, but I felt a twinge of pain in my side when I yawned. *Maybe it's my appendix?* I thought.

"You've been sleeping for about an hour. We're just south of the Beltrami State Forest."

I covered my mouth as I yawned again, and then inhaled sharply as the pain in my right ribs intensified. I felt better after sleeping, since I hadn't slept well the night before, but I still had an ache in my heart. Only that morning, I had left the Penner's house. Although they weren't related to me, they were the closest thing to a family I had.

Since Dad, I mean Keith, had admitted he wasn't my dad, and was put in jail, I stayed with his step-brother's family, the Penner's. After weeks of waiting, Mrs. Lyon found me a foster home in Iowa. I wasn't the least bit happy about leaving, but I was clinging to the verse that had become so special to me.

"Thou wilt keep him in perfect peace whose mind is stayed on Thee, because he trusteth in Thee," I quoted in my head. Yes, I was trusting God. Now if you know me, you also know that I am a new Christian and that a few weeks ago, I didn't care anything about anyone but me - sinful, proud, and selfish me. Then, God changed my life.

I looked at the clock. It had only been five hours since I said good-bye to my cousins and Uncle John and Aunt Amanda. It already seemed like a life time ago. I had only met Mrs. Lyon the day before, and now I was driving across the country with her.

We hadn't talked much, I had cried into my pillow for the first hour, and I guess after driving for so long, I had fallen asleep.

"Do you know the Tass family personally?" I asked, trying to make conversation. If I had to be stuck with a stranger in a car, I figured I might as well be polite.

"Of course I know them. That is why I knew that they would be so perfect for you," Mrs. Lyon replied in her sweet voice, that didn't match her facial expressions. "Tami, that's Mrs. Tass, teaches dance lessons, and she is the main singer in the Great Springs Rock Band. You will love her. She knows all of your favorite songs by heart."

"Mrs. Lyon, I don't think you understand. I'm not the same person that you were told about. I'm a Christian now, and I don't talk, or dress like I used to. I don't even listen to the same music that I used to."

"Oh, Amy, you don't have to play act around me. I talked to your friend Jennie, and I know all about you. You don't have to pretend you're a Christian around me. In fact, I deliberately picked the Tass family for you, because I knew that you won't have to pretend to be a Christian around them, they want you just like you've always been."

I stared in despair at the fields as they passed, Mrs. Lyon just didn't get it. I wasn't pretending to be different, I was different.

"What does Mr. Tass do?" I asked trying to change the subject.

"Mitch works for the government, and he's very wealthy. That is another reason I picked them for you. They can afford to buy you all of the latest gadgets, and the most popular clothes, and they can send you to the best colleges in the country. You will be put in a private school, and you will have every benefit of a millionaire's daughter."

"Money isn't everything, Mrs. Lyon."

"Of course it is. With all of the money that they have, they can have anything they want."

"But what will happen to them when they die? What is going to happen to you when you die?" I was surprised at my own boldness, but I figured that if I was going to have to drive half way across the country with a total stranger, I might as well make sure that she knew where I stood.

"Amy, you're a teenager, you're not supposed to worry about things like that. You're young, you have your whole life before you, don't waste it by worrying about death. When you get to Iowa, you will have the opportunity to be the most popular girl in your school. Don't ruin it by talking about things like religion. Nobody wants to hear about it. You should be worrying about what kind of make-up to wear, or where you want all those cute guys to take you out on dates."

"Mrs. Lyon, my question still stands, where are you going when you die? I would rather know where I'm going than be the most popular girl in the world."

"I don't feel comfortable talking about this but if you must know, I believe that when you die, that's it. You get buried, and that is the end. Now about the kids in your new school, I hear that there was already a boy asking about you."

"Mrs. Lyon, I mean no disrespect, but I don't care if every boy in the state was trying to take me out on a date. I would rather know that you were going to Heaven when you die."

"Like I said, when I die, I'm going into the ground, and that is the end."

"But what if you're wrong? What if there is a Heaven and a Hell, what then? Where will you go?" I pleaded.

"Let's not talk about that. Hey, when we get closer to Iowa, I want to stop at a clothing store, and we'll get you some more suitable clothes."

I looked down at my jean skirt and button up blue blouse with little flowers on it.

"What's wrong with these?" I asked.

"They aren't suited for someone of your new position. You want to fit in don't you? We'll buy you some stylish clothes, and you will most definitely need a new hair style. Maybe a Stacy Jensen cut or something. Then we need to get you some new makeup and accessories."

I sighed. All the expensive clothes and shoes that she was talking about used to mean the world to me, but now, I couldn't see why I had to be caught up in styles.

Mrs. Lyon glanced at me, and saw my serious face. "Look, Amy, I don't claim to know much about religion, but surely, you would be happier if you just dropped this whole thing. It would make life a lot easier for you if you just didn't have to pretend you're different from everyone else. You have the chance of a lifetime with the Tass family. Don't waste it by pretending to be something you're not. Just because you had some emotional experience once doesn't mean you have to wreak your life because of it."

I looked down at my hands. I wasn't pretending was I? I had changed hadn't I? But what if she was right? What if I had just had some kind of an emotional experience? I looked out the window at the passing fields. Was it possible to know if I really had changed? "How long till we stop?" I asked.

"There's a little steak house not too far from here, we'll stop there. It will probably be about ten more minutes."

I looked out the window again, and tried to sort out my thoughts. Houses started appearing here and there, and within minutes, we were in the small town of Bad Waters.

Dad had never spent much money taking me out to eat, so to me, this was a very fancy place.

When we got our food, I bowed my head and prayed. When I lifted my eyes, I caught the disapproving look of Mrs. Lyon.

"Amy, that kind of thing won't get you anywhere. You must stop praying or showing any signs of religion on the outside. The Tass family won't like that."

"But Ma'am…"

"Don't argue. I know them, and if you keep up this nonsense, they will not keep you, and then you will lose out on an opportunity of a lifetime."

"But ma'am…"

"What is wrong with you?" she interrupted again. "Just eat."

I prayed silently for strength. Was this worth fighting for? What if I just quit praying on the outside, would it really matter? Like a flash, Uncle John's words came back to me. 'Standing alone always takes courage Amy. I don't know when, but sometime, you're going to need to stand alone.' This was going to be hard. *God, please give me courage. I believe You when You said You'll keep us at peace, but I'm not at peace right now. What's wrong?* Then I remembered the rest of the verse. *Lord, please help me keep my mind stayed on You, so that I can have your perfect peace, and be able to stand alone.*

Standing alone. I liked the sound of that, but I knew I could never stand alone. Not on my own. *God, I need your strength.*

We ate in complete silence, I stared at my plate almost the whole time, and Mrs. Lyon looked everywhere except at me. I tried to eat everything on my plate, but I just wasn't hungry. I had been eating like normal, but lately I had been losing weight, and trust me when you weigh what I weigh you can't afford to just lose weight for no reason.

When we were done Mrs. Lyon paid the bill, and we started walking toward the car.

"Amy, get back!" a commanding voice yelled.

I recognized that voice, I started looking for the person speaking when he yelled again. "Amy, get down!" Without thinking I dropped to the pavement. Mrs. Lyon started to run for her car when four police officers started toward her.

"Put your hands on the back of your head and don't move!" Sheriff Trams yelled at her while holding his gun on her steadily.

I was in shock. *What is Sheriff Jim doing here?* I wondered. He was supposed to be back in Rifton.

Mrs. Lyon froze with a look of extreme disgust. The two female officers started to handcuff her as she protested her innocence.

"But, Sheriff Trams, you know me. I'm just taking Amy to her new foster home."

The officers ignored her pleas, and told her all of her rights. Then the two lady officers took her to the back of a waiting police car.

"Thank you for your cooperation," Sheriff Trams said turning to the other policeman.

"I'm just glad I could help," the other guy said, and I saw that he was also a local sheriff. His car said Sheriff of Bad Waters.

"Are you okay?" Sheriff Trams asked as he came over to help me up. When he helped me up I felt another stab of pain in my ribs. *Oh Bother*, I thought. I was supposed to be over that. Ever since my surgery a few years before I had had pain in my side off and on, and it seemed more often than not these days.

"Yes, Sir. I scratched my elbow a bit, but I'm fine," I said biting my lip to hide the pain.

"Good. Let me introduce you to Sheriff Anderson."

I reached out and shook Sheriff Anderson's extended hand.

"What just happened?" I asked in bewilderment.

"We just found out that Mrs. Lyon is wanted. Believe it or not, she was one of Steve's partners. He confessed that he had another partner, but he wouldn't say much of anything about her. Mrs. Lyon did some pretty smooth talking, and I didn't find out until after you left who she really was. We didn't catch up to you until right now."

"You mean Mrs. Lyon was kidnapping me?" I asked.

"Yes. She was trying to finish what Steve started. Steve is her brother. Anyway, I have found out so much in the last five hours that you have got to hear. Come on, I'll take you home."

The Sheriff grabbed my suitcase from Mrs. Lyon's car, and then we went to his car. He had said he was taking me home.

"Where is home?" I asked.

"That is what is so exciting!" he said. "I found out who your real parents are!"

# CHAPTER 2
# HOME 🚓

"Uncle John and Aunt Amanda are your parents!"

I froze.

"You don't seem happy?" Sheriff Trams said "Is something wrong?" He opened the car door for me, and held it open as he waited for me to answer.

"It's just that... well, Sheriff Trams, I love Uncle John and Aunt Amanda, but they're like my uncle and aunt. How could they be my parents?"

"You're their daughter Amanda that we all thought had drowned."

"How do you know that's who I am?" I asked as I tried to connect the dots in my head.

"Just a second." He shut my door and ran around the car and got in. He turned it on, and we took off. Then he continued. "I've been noticing ever since Uncle Luke got saved, that there was something he was hiding. He was doing a great job sharing his faith in the prison, but I always felt that there was something he wasn't telling me. So I asked him about it, and he finally confessed that he suspected you were really Amanda Penner. So I talked to Keith, and he finally confessed that he had been behind the Penner's house the day that little Amanda fell into the river. He saw her, and pulled her out. He took her to his house, and he kept her. He renamed her Amy, and moved away. Then he married, and was never caught until now. Amy, you are really Amanda Penner. Or as they called her, Manda."

"You mean my mom and dad stole me?" I twisted my fingers together. Why did the Sheriff think this was such good news? It was terrible news.

"Well, I don't know all the details yet. I only just found out shortly before we caught Mrs. Lyon."

"So you haven't told Uncle John yet?" I asked.

"No. I haven't had time. I need to talk to Keith again and figure out some more details, but I know that Uncle John would love to have you stay with them. Do you want to call him now?"

"No!"

Sheriff Trams jumped a bit at my harsh tone.

I sighed. "I'm sorry, but I don't know how I'm supposed to just walk into their house and act like I've always belonged."

"Amy. I thought you would be thrilled," he said. "I had no idea this would upset you, I thought you wanted to live with the Penners?"

"I do," I said trying to blink back the tears. "But when I think that my mom, must have known all along that I was kidnapped, it just makes it hard for me to think straight," I said putting my head in my hands. *How could this be?*

"Well, I don't know all the details, and until I do, I guess I don't have to tell them who you are."

"Oh please, Sheriff Trams, don't tell them. I'll tell them when the time is right, just not yet. Please?" I begged. Anything to stall my shocking news.

"I guess I can wait to tell them. But mind you, if you haven't told them by the time I get this all straightened out, I will tell them myself."

"Thank you, Sheriff Trams."

"I thought I told you to call me Jim?"

"You did."

"Then why are you calling me Sheriff Trams?"

"Because it seems natural."

"Well you need to break that habit. I'm Jim."

"Okay. Jim."

"That's better. Anyway, your Uncle Luke's court case was moved up to tomorrow. You will of course be expected to be there."

"I thought court cases were always slow, sometimes even happening years after the event?"

"They are in most places. But we don't like that around here, we believe in swift justice. So we try to have quick trials," he said reaching down and adjusting his seat. "We'll have you home soon," he said flipping on his lights and sirens, and speeding up.

"Is this allowed?" I asked glancing at the speedometer.

"Well, you can't drive this fast, but I am on a tight time schedule. I need to get back to my office and find out some more details."

I sat in silence. There was so much that didn't make sense. So many questions to ask. "Why was I so important to Steve? Why was Mrs. Lyon trying to kidnap me?"

"If I had to guess, I would say it had to do with a blackmail situation, but I don't know."

Time passed fast with Jim to talk to. He was almost like a big brother. After a few hours, we started getting close to the Penner farm. I felt like I could call it home. But then, home meant a place where a mom or dad lives, and when I thought of home, I thought of my mom and dad. I guess they really are my uncle and aunt. That thought startled me.

"Dad is really my Uncle Keith?" I asked

"Yes, Amy, your Uncle John and Aunt Amanda are really your dad and mom, and the man that you've always called dad, is your Uncle Keith."

I had to think about that for a bit. Uncle Keith just didn't sound right, and yet I no longer could call him dad. He wasn't what a father should be. Dads are supposed to care about their kids, not drop them off like mine did.

I slammed my fist down on the arm rest. Then realizing how much like Uncle Keith that was, I stamped my foot.

"Can you try not to brake my car?" Jim said.

"I'm sorry. I didn't mean to hurt anything," I said, and then I saw the slight smile on his lean face. "You're just teasing me aren't you?"

"I'm sorry, Amy. Yes, I was teasing you."

"I thought you said my D.N.A. didn't match anyone?" I asked trying to get him to stop smiling like everything was fine.

"And it didn't, but that just means that Uncle John has never been D.N.A. tested."

"I should be happy I know, but I just don't feel right. Keith is the only man that I have ever called dad, and I don't think I can call Uncle John, dad."

"I know how you feel, Amy. I didn't call my adopted dad, 'Dad' until I had lived with him for a long time. I know Uncle John, and he isn't going to try to take your Uncle Keith's place in your life. Uncle John will treat you like his other kids, and I know that he will love you and care for you as long as he lives, and in addition to all of that, he is the most godly and upright man I have ever known. He will help you grow spiritually, and he will always point you to your heavenly Father. What's so bad about all of that?"

"Nothing, I just don't know how to act around them," I said slowly. "I've always been a loner. I don't know how to deal with a family. I would feel more comfortable living in a place all by myself than with a big family. I just don't know how to act. After Mom died, I only had one friend."

"Nonsense, you act the same way you did before you knew who they were. Just be yourself. I'll keep my word. My lips are sealed, until I've got more details figured out. That may be today, it may be next week, and I would advise you to tell them before I do."

We turned into their driveway, and the familiar outline of the Penner's farm house came in view. The pine trees were still there at the end of the driveway, and the lawn was still just as big and welcoming. The barn stood in the back far corner, and everything looked cozy. Yet despite the home like feel, this wasn't home, and I wondered if it ever could be.

Jim got out and grabbed my suitcase. He still used his arm stiffly from when Dad, I mean Uncle Keith shot him.

"Are you going to sit in there all day?" Jim asked.

I got out wordlessly and headed up the steps toward the house that was supposed to be my home.

## CHAPTER 3
## OFF EASY 🚔

The Penner family was shocked beyond expression that I was back so soon. They thought that by now I would be half way to Iowa. But they were very glad to see me. I was greeted by hugs all around, and although I tried to restrain myself I couldn't help but cry tears of joy. I really did love this family.

That night at family devotions Uncle John read to us from the Bible, and then he closed in prayer. When he prayed, he thanked God for letting me spend more time with them.

"To think that we let you get in a car with a kidnapper…" Uncle John, I mean, Dad, said shaking his head. He seemed genuinely upset about it. I couldn't help but think how much more surprised they would be if they knew who I really was. They still thought that I was Amy Elwood.

"I guess you get the floor again." Grace said as she led me up to her room for the night. "Dad said that since you may be here for a while, he is going to have the guys bring in the top to my bunk bed. Then you can have a real bed."

"The top to your bed?"

"When we kids were little, Dad built a bunk bed on top of my bed, but he took it off after my sister died."

"Amanda?" I asked. *Me*.

"No. My other sister."

*     *     *

The next morning I woke up exited. I wasn't in Iowa, I wasn't being kidnapped. I was here with my cousins.

Then I remembered that they weren't really my cousins, but my siblings. I didn't say much during breakfast. All I could do was stare around the room at all these people who were really my family. I tried to put the name 'Dad' with Uncle John, and it didn't come too hard in my head, but I knew I would never be able to actually say it out loud.

Calling Aunt Amanda 'Mom' would be a little bit easier since I hadn't had a mom for so long, but even that seemed impossible.

Grace was without a doubt the closest thing to a sister that I had ever had. Timothy I guess would make an okay big brother, and I was already friends with Samuel and Philip. But then there was Paul.

I still hadn't been able to figure him out. He wouldn't speak unless spoken to, and when he did speak it was normally two words or less. And he looked at me funny whenever I was around.

"Amy, Jim wants you at the court case today, so if you can get ready in the next twenty minutes, we'll be leaving then," Uncle John said as he stood to leave the table. "And Amy…"

"Yes?" I didn't dare call him by name.

"I'm glad you're back." He smiled, but there were tears in his eyes.

What was it like for him to lose a child? Did I remind him of her? As I stared into his kind blue eyes, I wondered what he was thinking.

When we finally got to the court house, my hands trembled with nervousness. I didn't really want to be there, but I didn't really have a choice.

We sat in the very front. When Uncle Luke was brought out, I smiled at him, and he winked back. His once bitter and hard face was now just as calm and peaceful as Uncle John's face.

Uncle John, I mean Dad, got up and went over to talk to Uncle Luke and his lawyer, I saw Uncle John, I mean Dad, hug Uncle Luke, and I wondered what it must be like to have your twin on trial.

I didn't know whether the trial was going good or bad. If it had been a few weeks ago, I would have thought that he should go to jail for years, but now, I had seen the change, and I knew that if he could walk the streets today, he would never again be in trouble with the law. God had completely changed him, and I was proud to call him my uncle.

When the final court session started, I was completely unsure of the outcome. Like the sheriff, I mean Jim, had told me, Uncle Luke could get anywhere from several years to a few months. Depending on how the judge looked at his recent change of behavior.

There was a bit of whispering going on between the few spectators, and the room felt hot.

The startling sound of the judge's gavel rang through the room as it fell heavy on the desk. "Silence in the court room!

As you all know, the jury has found Luke Peter Penner guilty of attempted kidnapping." The judge paused.

I looked over at Uncle Luke, and saw him look down in shame. His attempted kidnapping was the only crime that they could actually pin on him. And although he had tried to tell the officers that he had done many other things including stealing and blackmail, the officer had basically told him that because he couldn't prove them he should just shut up and not make it harder for the court.

"In light of the fact that this is the first time Penner has ever been brought to court, and the fact that he now seems to be living on the straight and narrow road." The judge continued, "I see fit to make his sentence lighter than normal."

There was a long pause, and the room was deathly silent. I glanced over at Uncle Luke again. His head was bowed and his lips were moving. I knew he must be praying. When he raised his head, he had a calm and peaceful air about him, and I wondered if he knew my verse about being kept in peace when our minds are stayed on Christ.

His lawyer whispered something to him, and he nodded. I can't read lips, but if I had to guess what they were saying it looked to me like his lawyer asked him if he was doing okay, and he said he was prepared for anything.

"I hereby sentence you Luke Peter Penner to twenty-six months in jail or a fine of twenty-five thousand dollars. Which sentence would you like to fulfill?"

"Your Honor, in light of the fact that I don't have twenty-five thousand dollars, I will take the jail time." Uncle Luke's voice shook slightly, and yet he sounded resolved and almost happy.

"Before I pass final sentence, we have another angle we need to discuss," the judge said holding up a piece of paper. "On this paper, I have a letter from a man in this room, who as a teenager got in trouble and was sent to a juvenile detention center."

I looked at Uncle John wondering if he knew what this was about. But Uncle John and Uncle Luke were having a stare down. Uncle Luke had a look of complete disbelief, and Uncle John, had a sad smile that seemed to show a lot of love.

"It seems that the young man of whom I speak never served his time at the detention center, instead, his brother served his time for him. Since they are identical twins, the mix up was never caught." The judge cleared his throat. "Will Luke and John Penner both please rise."

# CHAPTER 4
# THINGS MADE RIGHT

I looked at Pastor John and his brother Luke as they stood, they both seemed so serious, and yet happy at the same time.

"Before I go on, John, is this really what you want? I mean you do have a family to think about." The judge looked down at Uncle John.

"Yes, Your Honor. I already discussed it with my family, and we feel that this is the best way to make up for the past."

"And do you, Luke Penner, have any idea what we are talking about?" The judge turned to Uncle Luke.

"Only vaguely, Your Honor, but if it is what I think it is, I vehemently oppose the idea. Yes, the past did scar me, but I regret nothing," Uncle Luke had a firm decided tone in his voice, and yet he also seemed somehow humble. It must have been his eyes.

"Well, it is no doubt what you think it is." The judge turned to the rest of the small audience. "For those of you who do not know this, in high school Luke Penner was sentenced to a juvenile detention center for his involvement in a robbery, in which a man was seriously hurt. Luke Penner went to the detention center, but he never committed the crime. His brother John Penner was the guilty party."

At this shocking news, I heard a lot of whispers behind me, and I looked up at Uncle John. He stood tall as ever, but a red hue had crept across his face. I couldn't help but notice the local newspaper reporter scribbling frantically in his notebook.

"Now as you all know, John Penner went to seminary, and is a very fine pastor. He didn't let the past stop him from becoming a great man. When he became a 'Christian' as he calls it, he confessed his wrong, but by then it was too late, his punishment had already been paid by his brother. And we are not here to discuss anything that John may have or may not have done. John Penner has offered to pay, or serve out the time that Luke Penner should receive."

"I'm sorry your honor, but I cannot allow my brother to spend over two years away from his family in a jail on my account," Luke interrupted. No one seemed to notice the fact that he was interrupting.

"Nevertheless, John has offered to pay the price for you. If he is still inclined, the court will allow him to pay the price." The judge looked back at Uncle John. "What sentence do you choose?"

Uncle John was silent for a few moments before he spoke. "I don't have the money yet Your Honor, but if I am permitted, I will earn it and pay the fine Your Honor."

"John, don't," Uncle Luke's firm voice argued. "You can't afford it. You have a family to support."

"Luke, this is my way of saying I love you, let's just let bygones be bygones." Uncle John replied.

"Please remain silent," the judge asked. "I hereby sentence Luke Peter Penner to remain in jail until John Paul Penner has raised the money he needs to pay the fine. Upon Luke's release, he will be assigned a parole officer, and will be required to check in at weekly intervals. He will not be allowed to leave the area for the first two months after his release, and he will have other restrictions. In addition, I ask that Luke Penner serve fifty hours of community service by working for John Penner on and at John's church. Court dismissed."

The ringing of the gavel on the desk shook me. I couldn't fully understand what had just happened, but from the looks on Uncle John, I mean Dad's face, and also on Uncle Luke's face, I knew it was good.

An officer came and started to escort Uncle Luke back to his prison cell when Uncle John, I mean Dad, got up and took off after them. I didn't want to be left alone, so I followed.

"Officer Will, can I have a moment?" Pastor John asked when he caught up to them.

"A very brief moment," Officer Will said stepping back. Uncle Luke and Uncle John threw their arms around each other, tears ran down their cheeks.

"You shouldn't have done that," Uncle Luke whispered huskily.

"I had to Luke. It's about time this community knows that you weren't involved in that robbery. I know this won't make up for all you went through, but I hope it helps. I'm very sorry for the past. Please forgive me?"

"Fully forgiven," Uncle Luke said playfully punching Uncle John in the arm. "I don't know how you will ever get that much money, but if you do, I will be eternally grateful."

As these two brothers stood next to each other, I couldn't see any visible differences in their looks, they were so much alike. I tried once more to call him Dad in my head. And it came a lot easier this time.

*I'll have to try that out loud sometime*, I thought.

"Sorry gentlemen, but we need to go," Officer Will said impatiently.

With one last hug, the brothers separated, and Officer Will placed his hand on the top of Uncle Luke's head as Luke got into the back of the police car.

"See you soon, Brother," Uncle John, I mean Dad said.

"I look forward to it," Uncle Luke replied.

Officer Will shut the door, and they drove off.

"Oh Amy, I've never been so happy in all my life!" Dad said hugging me. His embrace startled me, but I tried to act like it hadn't. "Let's go home and get the money," he finished.

"You have that much money just sitting around?" I asked, and then wished that I hadn't.

"No. I don't have that kind of money, but we'll get it," he said smiling. I immediately thought of how Uncle Keith would have gotten money if he needed it, and it bothered me. What if my Uncle John was just like that, what if he stole money too? I knew that he had as a boy, what was different?

Then I knew the answer, Uncle John, Dad, was a Christian. He served God, and he loved God, that in itself made him different.

I knew Uncle Keith would have never swallowed his pride enough to announce to the world that he had stolen money, and here Uncle John acted like being honest was the most natural thing in the world.

*Uncle John is exactly what I want in a dad*, I thought. I opened my mouth to tell him who I really was, but I bit my lip instead. What was the proper way to tell someone that you're their long lost daughter?

When we got home, Dad called a quick family meeting, in which he explained the outcome of the trial.

"So, what is the plan to get the money?" Samuel asked.

"Well before I talk, do any of you have any ideas?" Dad asked looking around the room.

"We could rob the bank?" Samuel suggested with a smirk.

"I'm serious," Dad said sternly.

"The most practical would be cattle," Paul said, and I almost jumped, to think that he had just said six words in a row! Maybe he would eventually learn to talk to me. Paul met my gaze, and I looked down. His deep brown eyes always seemed to bore holes into my head and I was sure he could read my thoughts.

"Actually, you took the words right out of my mouth," Dad said standing at the head of the table. "If we try hard, we may be able to get a load of cattle down to the auction today, but I don't know if that will be enough. Twenty-five thousand is a lot of money."

"You do realize that is our income for the next year don't you? If you do that, we may not be able to pay the bills for the next year," Aunt Amanda, I mean Mom, said with a look of concern on her face.

"I know that Dear. But God will take care of us. We won't starve, we may need to tighten our belts, but we can live without all the luxuries that we presently have," Dad said gently laying his hand on Mom's shoulder.

"What about your retirement account?" I asked, "Couldn't you just use some of that money?"

"An excellent idea for any normal family, but we aren't a normal family," Timothy explained. "You see, Amy, Dad and Mom don't have a retirement account. Their money is all in our livestock. If we need money, we just sell a cow."

"Well, I'd love to chat with you more, but we have work to do men," Dad said walking across the room and grabbing the phone. He dialed a number then waited.

"Hey, Billy, this is John. I was wondering how the auction is going?" there was a pause. "So if we left with a bunch we might have time to get down there before the auction's over?" there was another long pause. "Alright, that's great, we will see you then. Thanks a lot, Billy." Dad hung up, and turned to the guys. "Alright men," he said turning to the guys at the table. "Since we don't normally sell many cows in June, this is going to be kind of different. Timothy, I want you to pick out fourteen cow-calf pairs to sell, and any others that you don't think we need. Cull cows or whatever. I trust your judgment. Samuel and Philip will help you. I want them in the corral in one hour, don't worry if you can't get one, just leave it and go on. We're on a time schedule.

Paul, I want you to get the truck and trailer hooked up. I'll see if I can get a few more rigs, we'll need them. If we leave here in two hours, which is pushing it for time, we might be able to be there before the auction ends. We have a two hour drive, so move quickly, and don't waste time. Before we start though, let's have a word of prayer. Philip, would you lead us?"

Philip bowed his head and asked God to help them move fast, and to be safe. When he was done the guys left, and Dad got on the phone.

"Amanda," Dad said when he was done. "I need you and Grace to go get Dad's truck, and I want you to drop me off at the Reeble's place, I'm borrowing their truck and trailer as well. We should be able to get enough cows in the three trailers to make twenty-five thousand. That is, if they sell good. I don't know if we will even make it to the auction in time, so keep praying that we'll make it in time, and pray that they sell good." As Dad started for the door, with Mom and Grace, Dad saw me.

"Amy, could you pack us a lunch, and make sure that we have some water, we'll probably be gone for several hours. I know you don't live here, but just scrape together whatever you can find."

I didn't know for sure what I was supposed to make, but I managed to find a loaf of bread and some peanut butter and jelly, so I made some sandwiches and filled up some jugs with water. Then I sat at the table to wait.

I finally decided to try to call Jennie again, and talk to her about my whole parent situation, maybe she could help me. After all, she had been my only friend when I was growing up in Iowa. I hurried up to Grace's room, and grabbed my purse. I reached in for my cell phone, but my fingers brushed paper. Pulling my purse open wider, I saw an envelope. I pulled it out, and stared at the writing on the cover. It was addressed to me, in Uncle Keith's handwriting.

*The missing envelope.* I stared at it in shock. *Could it have really been here the whole time?* I wondered. Then I remembered. The larger envelope had been broken open, and in my hurry, I could have missed it.

I stared at it for a few minutes before I decided what to do, I mean if it had been a few weeks before, I would have opened it and read it without hesitation, but now, things were different, and I was different.

"There you are," Grace said coming into her room. "What have you got there?"

"This is the envelope that my dad left for me. I found it in my purse." I still couldn't bring myself to call Uncle Keith anything but 'dad' when talking out loud.

Grace paused, "Where did you find it?"

"It must have fallen out in my purse."

"Have you opened it?"

"No. I think I'll let Jim take care of it."

"I would be happy to give it to him for you," she said reaching out to take it.

"Why can't I?" I asked.

"Well, Dad wants you to go with him to the auction, so I thought maybe you would want him to get it before you get back tonight."

"You seem awful excited to see him?" When I said that, Grace turned red.

"Now, Grace, you're my sister," I paused at what I had just said. "I mean you're the closest thing to a sister that I have ever had," I bit my lip, why couldn't I ever say anything right? Sticking my chin out, I continued. "I want you to know that Jim is too old for you." I was almost frustrated, to think that Grace might actually like Jim. "He must be almost thirty!" I finished in a huff. "I'll give it to him myself." I shoved the envelope in my purse, and ran downstairs to the kitchen.

"There you are. John wants you in the barn yard right away, and make sure you bring the lunch with you," Mom said.

I grabbed the bags of food, and split them up between the three trucks.

"Timothy you take my truck and trailer, and head up the rear. You're the only one that I can guarantee is able to make it run," Dad said as Samuel and Philip loaded up the last of the cows. "Paul, you take Mr. Reeble's truck and trailer, I trust you to take better care of it than even I could."

Paul nodded, and I wondered what Dad saw in him that made him trust him so much, I didn't find him very agreeable.

"Amy, you come with me in Grandpa's truck. We'll take the lead." Dad ran around the truck and hopped in the driver's side, and I pulled myself up into the truck, there wasn't a running board any more, and since the truck was so high, getting in was hard. When I pulled myself into the truck, there was an intense pain in my side from the motion. I inhaled sharply through my teeth, then sat down and sighed.

Samuel was just locking up the last trailer when we pulled out of the driveway. Paul and Timothy followed us, and we went as fast as Dad dared to go with such a big load.

"Amy, do you know why I asked you to come along?"

"No," I said realizing for the first time that I was the only girl in the whole caravan of trucks. "Why did you want me along?" I asked.

"Amy, do you remember that conversation I had with you in the hospital room? You know, after you had jumped out of the barn?"

"How could I forget?" I muttered.

"Well, at the time, I didn't know what you were trying to say, but I understand you now, you were wondering if we would consider adopting you weren't you?"

He was right. He was a very blunt man. I normally liked his straight forward manner, but right now, I wished more than anything that he wasn't as smart as he seemed to be. "Well," he said looking out his window. "We tried to become your foster parents, but that didn't work." He glanced in his rearview mirror, anywhere but at me. "So, Aunt Amanda and I want to know if you would be willing to let us adopt you?"

# CHAPTER 5
# MISERY OF MISERIES 🚗

The view outside the window had never seemed so important to look at. What was wrong with me? I had begged God to make the Penners want to adopt me, and God had said no. Now that I knew who I was... I just didn't know what to think.

"Maybe this was a bad time to bring it up," Dad glanced at me.

I could hardly open my mouth. I knew that if Jim were there, he would have told me to tell Dad about who I was, but I just couldn't. So I just kept staring out the window.

"Did you hear me?" he asked. "Has something changed that you don't want to be with us now?"

I shook my head, and then nodded. Biting my lip I turned away and looked out the window.

"Is there anything that you want to talk about? I'm a good listener."

I shook my head again, and he sighed. I knew it hurt him, he actually loved me, and wanted me to be his daughter, and here I ignored him. But what else could I do? He didn't know that I really was his daughter.

"If you would rather be quiet, that's fine with me. But please, think about it. If we are going to adopt you, we need to start the process soon."

I didn't open my mouth. After several minutes of awkward silence, I reached into my purse for my cell phone, or anything to break the awful silence. Instead my fingers closed around the envelope.

I wanted to scream. Why couldn't I get away from my memories? I didn't want to be constantly reminded of my old dad, Uncle Keith. I had forgiven him, but it was still painful, the more I learned, the more uneasy I felt. For some reason, I had been very important to him, so important that he would risk his life just to get this envelope that I now held in my hand.

*If anyone has the right to open this envelope it's me,* I thought. *Besides, Officer Tony told me I could open it.* Maybe this envelope would tell me why everyone wanted to kidnap me. So with resolved fingers, I ripped open the envelope.

I had no idea how I had missed it in my purse, but I didn't really care.

I stared. Medical records? Then I saw it. The back sheet of paper held a diagram of my rib cage. In the middle of my right side, there was a rib colored bright red. But why was that important? I remembered having my rib replaced very clearly, and there wasn't anything important about that.

I flipped the paper over, and what I saw really shook me up. It was a diagram of a fake rib with a built in and sealed compartment in the middle.

*No wonder everyone is trying to kidnap me, they want to remove my rib and get whatever it is out of it,* I thought. But it still didn't make sense. I grabbed my cell phone, and called Jim.

"Is there any way that I can talk to Uncle Keith?" I asked when he said hello.

I noticed an odd stare from Dad when I called my old dad, Uncle Keith, but he didn't interrupt me.

"I take it that something is up?"

"Yes. I really need to talk to him," I replied.

"Well, Amy, I'm not at the jail right now, but if you can wait a little bit, I can call Officer Tony and have him hook Keith up to a phone and have him call you."

"That would be great. Thank you." And I hung up before he had time to ask me any more questions.

I felt bad about ignoring Dad, but he wouldn't understand. He didn't even know that I had a rib replaced because of an odd case of bone cancer. There was no way I was going to tell him either. I wasn't about to let him know about those painful memories. Just thinking about it made my side hurt.

I sat in complete silence for the next ten minutes until my phone rang.

"Hello, this is Amy?" I said.

"Why do you want to talk to me?" Uncle Keith snapped at me.

"Look, Jim told me the truth, about who I am." I glanced sideways at Dad to make sure that he didn't know what I was talking about. "I just found the thing that you almost killed yourself over, and I want an explanation."

There was a long pause and I wondered if maybe he had hung up.

"Are you still there?"

"Yes. Amy, I know you won't believe me, but I was trying to protect you the whole time."

"Protect me from what?"

"Well, when I took you, I saved your life. You were drowning, and I rescued you and then adopted you."

"Illegally," I added.

"Yes, Honey, we did break the law."

"But what about my rib?"

Dad gave me a weird look when I said this, and I realized that this might not have been the best place to make this phone call.

"Amy, the reason that I was so insistent on getting that envelope, is because if it falls into the wrong hands, then you will never be safe. Yes, I paid the doctor to put something in your rib, and if anyone else finds out about it, they will probably try to kidnap you to get it. Please trust me. I only did it for your good. I really do love you, and I'm trying to protect you from what will happen if everyone knows what you have."

"What do I have?" I asked.

"I can't tell you, Amy. If I told you, then you would be in danger. Look, my time is up and I have to go. Just remember that I really do wish you all the happiness with your real family, and I am sorry I took you. Tell your dad hello for me will you?"

"I love you," I said, but it was too late he had already hung up.

I didn't know what to do. This was obviously something really important, and it made me shudder at the thought of what Steve would have done to me had he gotten the opportunity. I guess he must have known that I had something special, but he didn't know what and he must have hoped that the envelope would reveal it.

I looked at the back of all the sheets of paper, and on the back of one of the other sheets, there was a note to me.

*Dear Amy,*

*If you ever need anything that money can buy, have surgery done, and remove the highlighted rib. What it contains will care for you when I can't.*

*Love, your Uncle Keith*

I stared in agony at the note. Uncle Keith had left me something, something special, something that only he and I knew about. Well I guess that Steve must have had some kind of an idea about it, or else he wouldn't have kept trying to have me kidnapped, but besides that, no one else knew.

I suddenly was aware of the fact that Dad was looking at the medical diagrams in my hand, and I quickly folded them up and stuck them into my purse.

Dad didn't say anything, and I didn't encourage conversation. Uncle Keith wanted me to go on with Dad and Mom and to not worry about him, but how was I supposed to do that? Uncle Keith had been a dad to me for so long, I didn't know if I really could let go. It was easy to let go when I remembered how he had treated me the last few times I had seen him, and how he hadn't wanted to talk to me when he was in jail, but when I thought of this last conversation, I couldn't even imagine that I didn't love him. He was trying to protect me.

I stared out the window trying to calm my thoughts and figure out what was going on. I didn't like any of the things that were going on, but then when had I ever liked my life? I had been happy with Uncle Keith, and Aunt Fay, but even my life then was shrouded in clouds. I didn't have any friends besides Jennie, and I had been in and out of the hospital more times than I could count. The only reason I wasn't a total outcast in school was because I could outrun them all. I had always been at the top of my track team.

I would have liked to have found out that my Uncle Keith was innocent, and that he really was my rightful father. I would have liked to have never seen him angry. I would have liked to have never seen the inside of a hospital. I would have liked it if I had never had to go to that crash scene and seen my Aunt Fay, hanging out of the broken glass window of that car. I would have liked to have never left my old home. But like I said, life never seems to go the way I want.

Why had my short life been filled with so much pain? I had felt so strong a few days before, but now, I felt nothing but defeat, I was all alone, everyone thought that I didn't belong to anyone, and to top it all off there was something in my rib that if the wrong people found out about, they would kill me without hesitation.

# CHAPTER 6
# THINGS JUST GOT WORSE 🚓

Dad was just about the happiest thing you could ever see when he came out of that auction barn with his check. It was for exactly twenty-five thousand dollars.

"Come on Amy, We're going home!" he said running around the truck to get the door for me.

I stood there staring at the open door. "Umm…" I didn't know how to say it, but after the awful trip there, I didn't want a repeat of it. "Is there any way I could ride in one of the other trucks?" I asked fidgeting with my purse strap.

Uncle John sighed. "I suppose if you want to." He paused. "I'm sorry if you're having a rough trip, Amy. Go ahead, Paul is a good listener."

I turned to go towards the other truck, and was met by Paul's stare. His dark eyebrows were lowered, and the corners of his mouth were turned down.

I sat in complete silence as I texted Jennie, she didn't answer any of my texts and I figured it must be because I had offended her somehow; probably when I had talked to her about the gospel. I had given my life to Christ and now, I didn't have any friends. Jennie had abandoned me. Grace was still my friend, but then, she was a part of my real family, and so even she was a reminder of how my life should have been. Nothing was right, and then Paul had to speak.

"Spit it out." Three words.

"Spit what out?" I asked.

He shrugged. "Whatever is wrong." Three more words.

"You wouldn't understand. You don't know anything about having your life messed up and thrown in your face. You don't know what it's like to be alone. You don't know what it's like to be unwanted, and hunted by every crook that happens to want money. And you don't know what it's like to lose your only friend." I ended in a huff, and immediately wished I hadn't said so much. But surely Paul wouldn't tell anyone about it. It would take him too many words, wouldn't it?

"You asked me why I didn't talk, and I told you that you reminded me of someone. That someone was my twin."

I froze, I had actually lost count of his words, but that didn't matter, what did he mean?

"You have a twin?" I asked in shock.

"I had a twin," he corrected.

"What happened to him?" I asked.

Paul paused for a while before answering, his lips were trembling. I suddenly felt bad for bringing up an unpleasant subject, maybe he didn't want to talk about it. Paul ran a hand through his black hair, and then began.

"My twin was a girl. Her name was Sylvia, the feminine form of Silas, it was Mom and Dad's hope that like Paul and Silas of old, Sylvia and I would serve God." Paul paused. He was chewing his bottom lip.

"Sylvia and I became Christians when we were six years old. For years we grew up reading our Bible together, memorizing together, and all kinds of other Spiritual things. But then when Manda drowned something changed in me, I started to get very angry, and argumentative. I didn't get along with Mom or Dad, and I blamed God for taking my little sister. I became very difficult to be with." There was another long pause, Paul's eyes held deep hurt.

"Three years ago, Sylvia helped me give it all to God. She wanted nothing more than to see me serve Him. Sylvia was always so strong for me." Paul smiled. "She developed such godly character, that she often put me to shame because of my selfishness. I mean she was the kind of girl that wouldn't go over the speed limit by even a mile even if there wasn't anyone else around. Wherever there was a chance to serve, she was always right in the middle of it. We were going to go on a mission trip together, but I got sick and insisted that she go without me. She never came home." Paul was back to his short choppy sentences.

"So where is she?" I asked.

"She's dead." Paul reached up and wiped a hand across his eyes. "There was a hurricane. The mission they were at was destroyed. Sylvia's team of eleven, were all there when it happened. Seven of them were killed instantly, and the other four, were all seriously injured. The couple leading the team was killed, and no one could identify any of them, so they flew the whole team back to the states where we family members were to meet them and identify them. We got word that the plane would land in Georgia, and the four living team members would be put in a hospital there. We flew straight there, but between the time that we got word, and the time that we got there, Sylvia's plane went down."

Paul ground his teeth together as he blinked back tears.

"Only six of the body bags were recovered, and three of the unconscious patients. There was no sign of our Sylvia." Paul chocked and looked away.

"After weeks of searching, we never did find anything. Sylvia was either in one of the missing body bags, or she was strapped to a hospital bed when the plane went down. Either way, she's dead."

"I'm sorry," I whispered.

Paul shrugged and set his jaw like stone.

"So that is why you never talk," I said slowly. "When you lost her, you lost your tongue too."

Paul shook his head. "Not really. When Manda drowned, I developed a rare case called psychogenic stuttering. It became very difficult for me to say anything without mixing up my words, and stuttering, it was a trial for anyone that I chose to speak to since they couldn't understand me. I finally decided not to talk at all." Paul sighed.

"When we were sixteen, and Sylvia left, I was forced to decide whether I was going to let all of these things make me bitter, or let them make me a better person. I wanted to blame God for taking away my sisters, and for taking away my speech, and for making me seem so dumb to everyone else. I couldn't even go to town because someone always ended up asking me a question, and I couldn't answer them in an understandable voice." Paul reached up to rub the bridge of his nose. His hand trembled.

"I didn't mind being basically mute when I had Sylvia because she could always understand me, but when she was gone, no one understood me. I couldn't even say my name right. I came to the place where I had to give it all to God and I had to tell God that if he never gave me my tongue back, than it was fine with me. I had to come to the place where I relied completely on God. When I got there, God slowly bit by bit started to take away my stutter. I'm nineteen now, and I've only been able to speak clearly for the last few months, but I still don't talk much out of habit."

"I'm sorry," I said again for lack of anything better to say. "I guess you do know better than most people what it's like to go through problems. I'm sorry. I was wrong, you really do understand pain."

"Your turn," he said.

I paused, what did he mean?

"I told you my side so that you would know that I understand you. Now why don't you tell me why you're hiding from us Manda."

I stared. Had he just called me Manda?

"Yes," he said answering my unanswered question. "I know you're my little sister. I knew it the first day I saw you."

"How?" I asked.

"Several things. You have a birth mark on your left wrist. You came out of nowhere into Uncle Keith's life at the same time we lost Amanda. You look just like Amanda would if she had grown older, and you look a lot like Dad."

"I do?"

Paul nodded. "Blond hair, blue eyes. You even have a slightly square jaw line."

"Does your whole family know?" I asked.

"No," was his short answer, but I no longer cared about the fact that he talked so little, I couldn't blame him. I just needed to reword my question.

"Does anyone else in your house know?"

"No. Timothy and Grace suspected it at first, but not anymore," Paul said. "They think that Jim would have figured it out if you were."

"He did. But I convinced him not to tell you guys until he knew more."

Paul glanced at me. "Why not?"

I bit my lip. "Because I'm scared of how I'm going to fit into your family." There, it was out.

"You won't fit in. But you don't have to. I don't fit in either."

"Thanks a lot," I muttered.

"It's the truth. You don't have to fit in, just find your little nick, and be yourself. In fact, I don't like it when someone has to conform to fit in. Be yourself, and never compromise."

"I suppose I should tell Dad and Mom who I am." I was surprised at how much easier it sounded to say mom and dad out loud than it had a few days ago.

"Well, you will need Dad's protection to make sure nobody finds out about your rib," Paul said causally.

# CHAPTER 7
# STUCK 🚓

Paul would never cease to amaze me. He knew everything.

"How do you know about my rib?" My nervous fingers instinctively twisted around a strand of my blond hair.

"It's obvious isn't it?" he said simply. I stared at him, he was actually serious.

Paul glanced at me, and sighed. "It's obvious there's something about you that's important. Nobody would just kidnap one girl over and over for no reason. Of course you knew where that envelope was, so they wanted you for that, but Mrs. Lyon knew that you hadn't found the envelope, and yet she still wanted you. Since you didn't have anything special with you, I figured that it must be something that you knew that no one else knew, but then I found out that you had surgery on your rib, and that Uncle Keith made a large deposit of money to a Doctor at that same time that had nothing to do with the normal hospital expenses. I just put two and two together and got four. You must have something hidden in your fake rib."

I was shocked, Paul was a brain. "How did you know that I had rib surgery?" I asked.

"They had to remove your rib when you had bone cancer."

"How did you know I had bone cancer?"

Paul shrugged. "I have my ways. I did a bunch of my own research."

The blinkers ahead of us turn on, and Dad pulled off at a gas station. Paul pulled up to a pump and got out. After he stuck the nozzle in the gas tank, he stepped back up to the door.

"You need to get out and talk to Dad," he commanded.

I shook my head. "I'm not ready yet."

"There's no time like the present. Manda, you need to do this."

"My name is Amy."

Paul shrugged. "Whatever."

"You are kind of annoying sometimes, you know that?" I said.

Paul smirked, and then nodded. "Get out."

I got out and went over to the truck that Dad was driving.

"Can I ride with you?" I asked.

"Hop in," he said as he put the nozzle back on the pump.

After he paid, he hopped back in the truck and we headed down the road.

"You get sick of Paul already? He normally doesn't talk enough to wear anyone out."

I didn't comment on that but secretly I felt a bond between Paul and me. Paul had just spoken more words than I think he had spoken at one time in years, and he had spoken them to me all because I reminded him of his twin.

"Amy, I'm sorry that I misunderstood you. I called your Aunt Amanda, and we discussed it, and since you don't seem to have any interest, we won't pursue adoption, since it obviously isn't what you want."

I bit my lip. How could I tell him now? He had given up on adopting me, and now I was supposed to tell him I was really his daughter?

I couldn't bring myself to open my mouth. Dad had given up on me just because I didn't say I wanted to be adopted. He hadn't been willing to fight for me. How could I tell him I was really his daughter? How was I supposed to tell him that I had a mysterious rib that every cutthroat in the state wanted? I could never ask him or anyone else to take the responsibility of protecting me.

Paul knew about my rib, but besides that no one else on this side of the bars did. And I was going to keep it that way. I tightly clamped my jaw shut and tried to make the muscles around it stop twitching. I was going to have to take care of myself.

"Amy, is there something on your mind?" Dad asked.

*How does he know when I'm hiding something?*

"No… Yes… I don't know." My fingers frantically twisted a strand of my blond hair.

"I've found that it often helps to share things with someone," he said when I hesitated.

"Let's just not talk about it. This is something that I need to work out." We were quiet for a long time. He didn't know what to say, and neither did I. I knew that he would make a great dad. I knew that he loved the Lord, but could I really trust him to care for me? Finally I could stand the suspense no longer.

"Dad, I need to talk to you." I had forced myself to say dad instead of Uncle John, but he didn't even seem to notice.

"I'm always willing to talk."

"I'm not really Amy Elwood," I blurted out.

"I know that," he said.

"But you don't know who my parents are, do you?"

"No. I don't. But I know that God is your Father, and I know that He loves you."

"Jim just found out the other day who my real parents are. But he promised to let me tell you if I did it before he did. Uncle Keith kidnapped me when I was drowning. I'm really your daughter, Manda."

There it was out. I let out my breath in a huff. I looked over at Dad for the first time, and the effect of my words on him was shocking.

He clenched the wheel so tight that his fingers turned white. He turned his head and stared at me. When he started to swerve, he pulled over. He ran his trembling hands through his short blond hair, and stared at me. I couldn't imagine what was going through his head. His face was a mask of shock, pain, and extreme love.

"Manda?"

I nodded.

"How? I mean…"

I reached out my left hand and pointed to my birth mark. He reached out, and gently took my hand. He gently slid his fingers over my birthmark, and then looked up, his eyes met mine, and tears began spilling down his cheeks. I don't know why, but if someone else is crying, I normally cry too.

Dad unbuckled his seat belt, got out of the truck, and came around to my side of the truck. As he opened my door, I undid my seat belt, and turned to get out assuming that that was what he wanted.

My feet didn't touch the ground. Dad threw his arms around me, and squeezed till I couldn't hardly breathe, but I didn't mind.

"Dad," I whispered just to hear how it sounded.

Dad leaned back and looked in my face. "My little Manda. My Dear Little Manda." Dad hugged me tightly again, and I hugged him back.

The other two trucks had pulled in behind us, and just then Paul and Timothy came up. Paul knew what was happening, and he was smiling like I had never seen before, his teeth were actually showing. Timothy had a puzzled look on his face.

"Is something wrong?" Timothy asked. Dad couldn't answer. He kept opening his mouth to say something, but he seemed to be choking on the words.

Paul grabbed Timothy and took him back behind the back truck. I'm guessing he was telling Timothy what was going on, and giving me a chance to spend time with Dad alone.

It was several minutes before Dad could talk, but when he did, I felt the love in his voice.

"You're my little girl." His voice was about three pitches higher than normal. "I did suspect it for a little while, but when Jim didn't say anything, I figured that it was just a desperate father's dream." He dashed his hand across his eyes before continuing.

"Jim didn't want me to get my hopes up, so he basically told me that my daughter was dead, and that he didn't have much hope. I just assumed that he already knew that you weren't related and so he didn't want us to get our hopes up. But you are really alive, and you're my little girl." Dad hugged me again, and I wondered why I had ever put off telling him. He was everything that I wanted in a dad and more. I couldn't help but love him. But there was still a shadow over me that wouldn't go away by simply feeling loved. I still had an ache in my chest any time I thought of Uncle Keith, or Aunt Fay, or the ever present reminder of my rib.

"Hadn't we best get going so that we can get your check cashed before the bank closes?" I asked.

"Of course." Dad started around the truck then he stopped walked back, and gave me another quick hug. It hurt my side when he hugged me, and yet I still liked it.

He firmly shut my door and ran around to the other side of the truck, jumped in and stared at me.

"Are we going?" I asked as I felt the heat rising in my cheeks under his steady and honest gaze.

"Right." He started the truck and took off. Every few moments, he looked at me with such amazement on his face that I didn't know what to think. There was a very noticeable silence in the truck. Dad was kept busy with watching the road and staring at me, and I didn't know what to say.

After what seemed like forever, I knew I had something else that I needed to tell him.

"Dad… There are some things about me that you need to know."

"Yes, of course. Please tell me all about yourself, I feel like I hardly know you. Tell me everything."

"I should have told you this before I told you that I was your daughter, but I'm afraid if I stay with you, you may be in danger. You see I have something that people want, and if anyone finds out that I have it, like Steve did, they will do anything they can to get it."

"No amount of danger can scare us off. It's my job as your father to protect you. I certainly won't let a little thing like danger keep me from you. I would rather call in full time body guards than lose you again. If you just give me whatever this thing is that you have, we can put it in a safe place."

"It's not that easy, I can't just give it to you for safe keeping. You see, it's in my fake rib." The look that he gave me was worthy of the 'Non-comprehension look of the year' award. I mean, he just didn't seem to get it.

"You own a fake rib? Like the kind that you would get off of one of those scientific skeletons?" he asked.

"I mean that I'm missing a rib, and I have a fake one in its place. In order to get it you would either have to perform surgery, or kill me."

His eyebrows raced for his hairline, "You mean you have something valuable in one of your ribs? What is it?"

"I don't know. All I know is that it must be very valuable from everything that Uncle Keith wrote. You see, I found that envelope in my purse, and it tells some about it, but not much."

"This is a little hard to comprehend. You're telling me that you lost a rib, and had it replaced with a fake one that has something valuable inside of it? It would have to be an incredibly small thing."

"That's what I'm saying," I replied.

"What happened to your rib?"

That was one question that I had no desire to answer, I didn't want to think about those awful weeks, let alone speak of them, and yet, I felt that I really ought to tell Dad. I knew better than anyone that you can't have a good relationship with someone unless it's an open relationship. I took a deep breath then began.

"About three years ago, I had a lot of pain in my rib cage whenever I ran. I loved to run, but I got to the place where I could hardly run without pain. I passed out a couple of times, and my coach made me quit the track team. I went in for some checkups, and the doctor took some x-rays and other tests. They found out that I had bone cancer in three of my ribs on the right side of my rib cage." Now it was my turn to look away in pain.

"They started to do treatments, and besides the fact that I lost my hair, and was sick for weeks, it wasn't that bad. Then they told me that most of the cancer was gone, but there was this one rib that was too far gone to save, so they removed it, and replaced it with an artificial rib. I went through several rounds of treatment, and the doctor told me that I was cancer free. From what he could tell, he said I should never have trouble with it again." I paused as I remembered those weeks in and out of the hospital. I could still feel the burning of stomach acids in my throat, and I could still remember the laughing of the kids at school when I went bald.

I could still smell the hospitals anti-germ smell, and I could still remember the pain in my side as I recovered, I would never forget the burning and the numbing pain, and the helpless feeling of not being able to do anything for myself. I would never forget the bad memories of those awful months.

"I guess Uncle Keith must have paid someone a lot of money to get something valuable put into my rib." I tried to sound like everything was normal, but even thinking about my time in the hospital made me shudder.

"Maybe it would be safest for you if we had your rib removed and replaced with a less valuable rib. We could then know what was inside your rib, and we could also protect you easier if you weren't walking around with all of that value in your rib. So maybe we should just remove your rib…"

"No!" I think I was almost yelling. There was no way I was going to go through all that pain again. I had never fully healed, and I still felt pain in my side whenever I did something at all strenuous "Whatever is in there is going to stay there till the day I die," I said firmly.

"Is there something you're not telling me?" he asked.

"It's just that I don't want to even think about the pain of going through all of that again." Tears came to my eyes, and I tried to wipe them away before they were seen, but it wasn't enough. Dad noticed my tears and reached over and gently squeezed my shoulder.

"Amy, you can trust me. I won't put you through anything like that without your consent. I love you. Let's just keep quiet about it. How would anyone find out anyway?"

"I don't know, but Steve knew, and Mrs. Lyon knew. What's to stop someone else from finding out?"

"I don't know but…" Dad slammed on his brakes.

In front of us a semi-truck coming around a corner, turned too sharply and its trailer tipped, spilling its load of logs all over the highway.

Dad stopped the truck, and got out to see if everyone was okay. He came back to the truck in less than a minute.

"The driver's fine and he's calling someone to get his load, but we can't get past him, and it probably won't be fixed for at least another hour, if we wait that long, we won't have time to get to the bank."

"Can we take a detour?" I asked.

"I'm afraid the only one that I can think of that would be at all passable would waste over an hour. We're stuck."

"Why can't we just wait until tomorrow? Uncle Luke will still be there?" I asked.

"We could, but I promised Luke that I would get him out, and I don't want to make him wait, he has already spent too much time in jail on my account."

"What happened? I mean how did you get in trouble with the law, you're a pastor?" I asked.

Dad sighed. "Do you really want to know?"

# CHAPTER 8
## A REUNION 🚓

Timothy came up to Dad's window and asked him if there was any way that we could help. It didn't seem like it, so Timothy went back to his truck.

"You asked me about my past, Amy, or I guess I can call you Manda. Which would you prefer?"

"I'm Amy. And I always will be. Amy could be short for Amanda just as much as Manda, so if no one cares, can I just keep being Amy?"

"That's more than alright, Amy. Anyway, when we were little kids, Luke and I were so much alike that even Mom had trouble telling us apart. We dressed the same, we talked the same, we did all of the same things, we acted the same. But somewhere in our early teen years, we started to not get along as well. I mean we still dressed the same, and did our hair the same, but I started to hang out with a different group of guys, and Luke didn't want to. I made fun of him, and told him that he needed to get a life, but I realize now, that he was right. I didn't care about spiritual things. I didn't care about much of anything but being popular. It was my way of dealing with my dad's death, and my mom's new marriage."

"I know what that's like," I muttered under my breath.

"Anyway, one day, I went out with my friends, and we decided to rob the local gas station. It was closed that night, and so we thought we could get away with it, but someone came in and one of the guys knocked him on the head, and when an alarm went off, we left. I ran home, and quickly changed my clothes, and sat down in my bedroom with a cup of coffee and a movie. The police came to the house with a picture of me from the security camera. They were about to arrest me, when Luke came in the room, he was dressed just like I was in the picture, and since I looked like I had been in the house all evening, they arrested Luke." Dad looked down in shame.

"I'm as sorry as I can be for that, I was very wrong. Luke spent a year in a detention center for what I did. I finally got my heart right with God, and when I did, I went to the police and told them what had happened; they said it didn't matter, since the crime had already been paid for. Luke wouldn't speak to me after that," Dad sighed.

"He had always been the good kid, and I ruined his name. While he was in Juvie, he got hooked up with the wrong crowd, and he never really straightened out after that, until now."

"But how did you become a Christian?" I asked.

"I always thought that I was saved when I was growing up, because I had said a prayer as a kid, but I didn't really know what it was all about. I didn't realize that Jesus died to pay for my sin. I had always just kind of thought of Jesus as another thing to add to my list of reasons why I was such a good person. Mom tried to make me see the truth, and when she remarried, my step-dad tried to help me as well, but I was blind. Mom wanted me to become a pastor, and even though I wasn't really excited about it, I wanted to get out of the house, it was too painful living with Luke and not being able to speak to him, so I left, and went to college, that's where I really understood Jesus, and that is where I committed my life to Christ. It was actually your mom that got me to see my problems."

"She went to college to be a pastor?" I asked in shock.

"No, she lived nearby, and helped in the kitchen. I got committed to God, and ever since, I've been trying to get in contact with my brother Luke, but he left, moved to California, and got married."

"Uncle Luke is married?" I asked.

Dad nodded, "He has a son as well, but I don't know much about his family. From what I understand, he left his family about three years ago, and has been running around the country doing odd jobs, and trying to get money without being put in jail. He fell into the wrong company again, and that's why he's where he is now. I guess I feel like it's my fault that he's where he is today."

"I'm sorry, I'm glad that you can make things right though."

"I'll never be able to make things right. I've done too much damage. The fact that Luke is willing to be my friend again, is all of God. If it weren't for God, I wouldn't be able to live with myself. But God is good, and He forgave me, and now I'm His child. It is good to know that I'm God's child, but I still make mistakes. I know Luke has a lot of problems from being blamed for my wrong, and I intend to do what I can to make it right, which is why I need to get this money to the bank right now." I saw a light come into Dad's eyes, and he jumped out of the truck and strode up to where the truck driver was talking with an officer who had stopped by to make sure no one was hurt. I could see him talking, and then he ran back along the line of our trucks, and got Paul and Timothy and some other guys that must have been waiting in vehicles back there as well.

Dad's slightly square jaw was set in determination and his blue eyes were narrowed to slits. He looked really tall and powerful as he strode past the truck with the other guys.

Dad flexed his muscles, bent down, and lifted one end of one of the logs. They were more like trees, and Timothy grabbed the other end with Paul lifting in the middle, they managed to lift the log just enough to move it a few feet.

"Will this help?" another guy yelled as he came up to them pulling a chain.

"That's perfect," Dad said. They lifted it again, and they slid the chain under it. After tying it off, Dad unhooked our trailer and wrapped the chain around his hitch and pulled it to the side of the road. The more times they did this the faster they got, and they managed to pull enough of the logs off of the road to make one lane semi passible. (I wouldn't have called it passible at all, but Dad was sure he could make it.)

After hooking up the trailer, we started to slowly crawl through the small gap. We were half in the ditch, but we made it through, and Timothy and Paul made it through without any trouble as well.

We didn't have time to go back to the farm, so Dad and I went straight to the bank. Dad ran up to the bank and pushed open the door. The guy was just locking up, but I saw Dad pleading with the man, and in a few minutes, they walked out of sight, and went into the bank. After about five minutes, Dad came out with a large envelope. He was grinning from ear to ear, and I knew they must have let him get the money.

"To the jail," Dad said as he got into the truck. He couldn't stop smiling, and I couldn't help but feel happy too. That's something about my dad's face that you have to understand. When he's frowning, he looks like a very hard and scary man. I think it's because of his square jaw. But when he smiles, his blue eyes and blond hair frame his face with an almost angelic appearance, and it just about makes you have to smile too.

When we pulled up to the jail, Dad jumped out, slamming his door behind him, and strode towards the front door. I followed, and I felt very weird walking into that front reception room. The last time I had been in there was not something that I wanted to remember.

Dad was already down a hall and in some office when I got in there, and so I just sat down in the front room.

"Did you tell them yet Amy?" Jim came up beside me, he had an envelope in his hand, and he looked like he was on the run like usual.

"I told Dad."

"Good! I knew you would. Now, I just found out something that might interest you. Your Uncle Keith had a large deposit in a bank in Detroit. Three years ago he took it out and bought gold with it. He says that he buried it and left you a map. I think maybe that's what your mysterious envelope is all about."

"I'm sorry Jim, but I don't think so." I reached into my purse and pulled out the envelope, "This is what the envelope contains, I found it earlier today."

Jim took it and studied it for a little bit. Then he handed it back.

"Grace told me that you had found it, but that doesn't make much sense to me."

"I have a fake rib," I said, "It has a secret compartment. Maybe the map is in there?"

"It doesn't really matter. The money he used to buy the gold with was stolen. We may need to remove your rib and find the gold so that we can pay back the guy that it was stolen from."

"If at all possible, I don't want surgery."

"Of course you don't want your rib removed, so we will try to avoid it. With that information though, I may be able to get some more leads. Anyway, Grace said that you were awful touchy about the envelope. I understand that it's special to you with that note on it from your Uncle Keith, but I don't know if it is a good idea to have such information where everyone can steal it. How about we put it in the vault here? Then no one will have any way of knowing which rib to remove."

"Go ahead and keep the envelope, I don't ever want to see it again." Then I remembered Grace. "And it seems that Grace sure tells you a lot these days."

He smirked.

I basically put my finger in Jim's face. "Stay away from her. You don't know her that well, and you're much too old for her, and if that isn't enough, she's my sister, we don't want to break up the family."

The looks on Jim's face as I finished my spiel were priceless, first amusement, then worry.

"Do you really think I'm too old for her?" he asked. I was shocked, he had actually thought about her!

"Of course you're too old, you're like nearly thirty, and she's only twenty. Besides, you wouldn't really consider marriage. It would wreck your career as a sheriff." I was very firm and rather shocked at the whole matter, to think that Jim had actually thought of marrying Grace!

"Actually, Grace is twenty-three, and I'm only twenty-nine, we're only six years apart."

"Forget it. Grace is such a godly woman and I want to get to know her, I want to be friends with her, and you can't marry her."

Jim lowered his voice to a whisper and stepped closer to me. "This is a secret, but I've already asked your dad for Grace's hand in marriage." Jim was grinning like he had just won the moon. "I know your dad has a lot going on right now, but I just felt that it was God's time."

"Dad said no, right?" I asked.

"He hasn't actually gotten back with me, but last time I talked to him, he seemed very hopeful." Jim had a very childish grin on his face and I wondered what this world was coming to.

"Hey, keep quiet about that will you? And by the way, I really need to go." Jim rushed down the hall, with the envelope, and entered his office that had big windows facing the front room.

I tried to picture Grace and Jim together, but it just didn't work.

I waited for a while, and eventually Dad came back with Uncle Luke. They were both grinning, and they both had tears in their eyes. When Dad saw me, he put his arm around me.

"Do you remember hearing about how our little Amanda drowned? Well this is her, she didn't really drown. Keith took her."

Uncle Luke winked at me. "I'm so glad to know that you are going to be in a good Christian home, I feel so bad about everything I did to you. I know you've forgiven me, but if there is ever anything that you need, I'll always be willing to help you," Uncle Luke said with such a genuine tone that I knew I could trust him, even his voice was the same as Dad's.

"Uncle Luke, can I have a word with you in private please?" Jim asked as he stuck his head around the corner.

"Yes, Sir," Uncle Luke said turning to go into Jim's office.

"Oh, Amy, you can never know how happy I am," Dad said putting his hands on my shoulders and looking me in the eye. "Two of the people in my life that I was sure I would never see again, God has restored to me! When you left, I felt that it was my fault. But God has given you back, and I am so happy." His face was glowing, and I couldn't help but smile back.

When Uncle Luke came out of Jim's office, he had a very serious expression on his face, and yet he was still smiling.

"Let's go," Dad said holding the door open for us.

When we got to the truck, Dad didn't take us straight home like I expected, instead, he took us to a small clothing store.

"For old times' sake, Luke," he said getting out. Uncle Luke followed him, so I followed too. Dad picked out two pairs of new jeans and two identical polo shirts. He then started down a guy's shoe isle, and I took off for the ladies clothes, I wasn't about to spend my day looking at men's stuff. When Dad was ready to leave, he paid for his purchases, and we headed out the door.

"Amy, you can wait in the truck," Dad said as he and Uncle Luke walked over to the gas station next door. When they walked out of that gas station, I didn't know who was dad and who was Uncle Luke, they stood side by side waiting to hear what I thought, but I didn't know what I thought. They were identical, even their watches were the same. Their hair was combed the same way, their hands both hung by their sides in the same fashion, and they had their feet in the same positions.

"Wow. How am I supposed to tell you guys apart?"

They looked at each other and laughed.

"I have a slightly higher ridge on my nose and my jaw is slightly squarer," the one of them said, but that didn't help me since they sounded the same, I couldn't even tell that his nose was more defined. Then I knew it, I looked at their hands, and I knew immediately who was who. Dad had a wedding ring on, Uncle Luke did not.

They told me that I was right, but I wouldn't be able to use that for long because Uncle Luke was going to put on his wedding ring as soon as he got it back.

"Let's go home. I need to tell Amanda about our Amy," Dad said heading for the driver's side of the truck.

"Nice truck," Uncle Luke commented as he let me into the back seat.

"It's actually Dad's truck," my dad said.

We got home, and I was met by hugs from everyone. My side hurt more with all these hugs than it had hurt for a very long time, but it was worth it. Timothy and Paul had told them about me. Mom was especially emotional over me, and it made me feel awkward, and yet it was a good kind of uncomfortable feeling. I had never felt so loved in all my life. But there was still a very dark cloud hanging over my head, my rib.

# CHAPTER 9
## IT JUST DIDN'T WORK🚓

That night at supper, we had a little bit of a celebration supper. I was home from the dead, Uncle Luke was home from who knows where, and we invited Grandpa and Grandma Elwood as well. They were very happy to see Uncle Luke.

But to my mortification, there was another guest as well… Jim. Dad had given him his blessing, and Grace had accepted. They were going to be married. No, they weren't engaged yet, but they had a marriage commitment. I didn't know why I wasn't happy about it. Jim was like a brother to me already, and I wanted Grace to be happy, but something didn't seem right. There were clouds on the horizon. I could feel it.

Uncle Luke called his wife. He had tried several times since he had gotten saved, but he hadn't gotten a hold of her yet. Well that night, she answered her phone.

When Uncle Luke got off the phone, he looked ten years older, his smirk was gone and his face looked haggard.

"Do you want to talk about it, or is it something that you would rather not discuss?" Dad asked.

"I think I need to discuss it," Uncle Luke said. He took a deep breath, and ran his fingers through his hair. "I'm afraid

I've done too much damage, Susanna doesn't trust me, and I don't blame her. I did just leave her and Travis... Even though we never divorced, she feels like we did, and she has been visiting another guy. She says it isn't serious yet, but she said unless I prove myself, she will divorce me and marry him. She doesn't believe that I've changed. I tried to share the gospel with her, but she didn't really seem to understand."

"How are you supposed to work on it if she doesn't trust you or want to see you?" Mom asked.

"I guess that's where the good news comes in. She said if I paid for the tickets both ways, she would let Travis fly out to visit me. She said that if he came home with a good enough report, she would consider getting back together and working on things. The only problem with that is that I don't have the money to buy plane tickets."

"I'm afraid I can't help you with that," Dad said. "You've about cleaned me out of my last dollar."

"We'll help," Grandpa Elwood said calmly.

"Dad, I would never ask you to buy tickets for my son to come visit me," Uncle Luke said.

"Of course you wouldn't, but that doesn't mean that I wouldn't offer it. You're forgetting that I've never met my grandson. I insist that you take the money," Grandpa said putting one of his large wrinkled hands on Uncle Luke's shoulder. "And by the way, son, I'm glad you're free."

Uncle Luke hugged Grandpa, and I remember thinking how they were so much closer than a lot of real father and son pairs were.

"And we are so excited to have you home Amy," Grandpa said including me in all the attention. I didn't want to be the center of attention, and yet it felt so good to be loved, and cared about.

As I lay in bed that night, there was a soft knock on my door.

"Come in?"

Mom walked in and smiled down at me. "Oh Amy, it is hard to believe that you really are alive and well, after all those years of thinking you were dead."

"Didn't you ever suspect that I might really be your daughter?" I asked. Now that I knew, it seemed so obvious.

"I always wondered if maybe my little Amanda was still alive. But it hurt almost worse thinking that she was out there somewhere, than knowing that she was dead. When I first saw you, I thought it was a possibility. But somehow, hearing you call Keith, 'Dad,' made it seem like you belonged to someone else. When Jim told me he was trying to find your real family, I knew that if it was us, he would have figured it out. When he didn't say anything, I just assumed that I must have been dreaming, and hoping. But now you're here," Mom said as she smoothed out the quilt on Grace's bed with her hand. I noticed that her hand was trembling.

"I'm glad to be back too," I said. Now that I had told them about myself, I realized that it would all be for the best.

"To think how close we were to losing you again, when Keith and Steve had you, and again when Mrs. Lyon had you. I know you may never be out of danger, but I don't think I could bear losing you again. John told me about your rib, and we discussed it briefly with Jim. Since we don't know for sure if Keith was even telling the truth, we aren't going to have your rib removed again. If there is anything there, then we'll live without it, and if there isn't, there is no way we would want to put you through that."

"Thank you, Mom," I said. There was no way that she knew how much I had been through, and yet she loved me enough to be able to know that I didn't want to have surgery.

"Would you mind going with Grace to town in the morning? She's planning on stopping at Jim's office and visiting him, and I thought you might like some one on one sister time."

"Oh thank you, Mom. That would mean a lot to me." I said.

*　　*　　*

"You look fine," I said looking over her shoulder.

"I have to look just right." Grace said as she stared into the mirror.

I rolled my eyes. "If you're going to marry Jim, he had better not care if you have one little hair out of place."

Grace didn't seem to hear me, but instead she tucked a wisp of her dark hair behind her ear.

"Are you ready to go?" I asked.

Grace stared in the mirror for a second longer. "I guess."

"Good, let's go." I led the way down stairs, and out to their car.

"I don't even know why you need me along, but I'm glad to be able to come with you."

"Well, Amy, I have this commitment that I will never touch a guy in a special way except for my husband, and that won't be until after we're married. The Bible says that it is good for a man not to touch a woman. Jim has the same commitment, but our parents think that it is wise to never be alone with each other until we are married. It will keep us accountable. So that's why you're here. You are our chaperone."

"Huh," I said, "I'll have to think about that."

Jim was sitting behind his desk talking very fervently with another gentleman when we arrived. He didn't notice us when we entered the front room.

"We should wait until he's not busy," Grace said sitting down. I snorted.

"Jim will never be done with his work," I said. But I sat down by Grace to wait. I couldn't help but stare at how beautiful Grace was with her wavy dark hair framing her face and soft brown eyes. I was proud to be her sister. It's no wonder Jim liked her.

A few minutes later, the man that had been in Jim's office darted out and fled the building. He didn't walk, he was darting. He obviously didn't want to be seen coming out of the Sheriff's office.

Grace stood up, and I followed her. She tapped on the door jam, and Jim looked up. The moment he saw who it was his careful and overworked look fled, and was replaced by a cheesy grin.

"Come in," he said standing and pulling out a chair for her to sit on.

"I bought these for you," he said picking up a dozen roses from the counter behind him. Grace turned an even brighter shade of pink, and I couldn't help but feel awkward just being there.

"Oh, Jim, they're beautiful!" Grace said as she buried her nose in the roses.

*Oh, Jim? Oh brother.* I stepped out of the room, and walked over to where I could see in his big window from the front room, but I didn't have to listen to their mushy talk.

When the outside door opened and someone came in, I jumped. My last experience with someone coming in that door wasn't very pleasant, but this time, it wasn't Uncle Keith or Steve. Instead it was a very short and very thin middle aged woman in a suit jacket.

"I need to talk to Sheriff Trams," she said, her heels clicking as she walked up to the front desk. I couldn't help but notice her brief case, and I figured that she must have a lot of business with Jim, and it was my job to make sure that Jim and Grace got to talk. So I stood to my feet, and planted myself in front of his office door. When the business woman came towards me, she looked right past me like I was a part of the door frame.

"Excuse me, but I need to see the Sheriff," she said.

"I'm sorry, but the Sheriff is in a very important meeting already," I said firmly. "You'll just have to wait."

"Amy," the secretary at the front desk called to me.

"Yes, ma'am?"

"You need to let Miss Jensen into the Sheriff's office."

Suddenly it clicked. Miss Jensen wasn't married, and she was much closer to Jim's age, and she was also very beautiful, and she had business with the Sheriff. Every misgiving I had about Jim and Grace vanished. What was I thinking? They were perfect for each other, and they were going to get married if I had any say in the matter. I felt myself getting mad at this woman. But I knew that I needed to let her in, so I opened Jim's door, and let her in, but I firmly planted myself inside his office with my back to the shut door. No one was going to hurt my Grace as long as I was there.

"Sheriff Trams, I think it would be best if I spoke to you in private," she said sweetly. I tensed.

"Miss Jensen, this is Grace Penner, and she is going to be my wife, I have no secrets from her." I felt like giving Jim a round of applause.

"Very nice to meet you," Miss Jensen smiled at Grace, and took a seat across from Jim. She set her brief case on the desk and opened it. She pulled out four file folders and handed them to Jim. The room was very quiet except for the rustling of paper as Jim scanned through the different folders. He looked through each one with deep interest, and then he looked up.

"What do these files have to do with me?"

Miss Jensen smiled sadly. "I don't want to remind you of your painful past, but I need you to tell me about your mom."

Jim stiffened. His face turned a slightly lighter shade and he stood up and turned his back on us as he stared at a painting on the wall.

"I don't know that much about my mom. Except that she was only sixteen when she had me, and she left when I was three months old. Of course I have no memories of her."

"I know this isn't something that you want to remember, but I need you to think back to what you know of her. Did your father ever mention what her name was, or anything like that? Maybe where she lived?" I sensed in Miss Jensen a very kind and compassionate attitude, very unlike what I had first assumed about her.

Jim turned back to us. "I do remember Dad talking about her once, I even remember where he was standing in the house, and I remember him saying her name. But I don't know what it was any more. I was only five years old at the time. I remember that it started with a T, or something like that, no maybe it was a K? I don't know."

"Was it by any chance Teresa Konley?"

Jim's head shot up, his face turned a shade whiter, and he nodded. "That's the name." Jim placed a hand on his desk for support. "But what does she have to do with anything?"

"I hate to be the one to tell you this, but she just died."

Jim's jaw tightened, but besides that I didn't see any visible signs of emotion. "How?" was all he asked.

"It was a deliberate drug overdose."

"Thank you for telling me," Jim said calmly, but I could see that deep look of responsibility and pain return to his brow. He once more looked like he was an old man with too much to worry about.

"I'm afraid that wasn't the only reason I came. You see, from my department's research, seven years after she left you and your father, when she was twenty three years old, she married a man in Chicago. They were married for six years, and had three children. She then left him, and several years ago, she moved to Des Moines and had another child. No one but her knew who the father was. This is a copy of her suicide note." Miss Jensen handed Jim another piece of paper. I couldn't help but feel bad for her. I knew that she didn't like the news that she was telling him.

Jim's eyes scanned the paper, and his eyes got wider as he read. His face turned about ten shades whiter, and he sat down heavily in his chair. He stared at the note for what seemed like forever before he looked up with questioning eyes.

"Those files I gave you are your half siblings. The two oldest ones are old enough to not need a guardian, but they aren't able to be a guardian, and they won't leave their sibling. So if you choose to be his guardian, you will also get the older two. And as for the younger one, she has been living in a foster home all of her life. It took quite a bit of tracking to find her. It's a good thing her name was on that piece of paper otherwise we would have never found her," she said motioning toward the suicide note. "We've contacted her foster home, and they are willing to let you have custody if you want it. I realize that this is a big decision, so I'm going to leave and let you think about it. But I leave for St. Paul in the morning and I need to know by then if possible."

"Thank You, Miss Jensen. I appreciate you telling me all of this," Jim said standing up again, but he didn't look well enough to stand.

"Not at all. You can keep that copy of the note, and those files for now. They might help you decide." She set a business card on the desk, then turned and left.

The moment that Miss Jensen was out of the room, Jim fell back into his chair, his forehead was wrinkled, and he was a very light pale color. He put his elbows on the desk and propped his chin up on his hands while he stared at the folders on his desk. I wondered if he even knew that we were there.

Several minutes went by before he spoke.

"I'm afraid I won't be able to marry you, Grace."

I jumped a bit at his harsh words. But my reaction was nothing like Grace's. Her face pinched into a hard sad look, and she stood to her feet and walked over by him. As she stood there with her dark hair cascading around her, and her pale face, she reminded me of what a martyr must look like when sentenced to death.

"Jim, we can work this out," Grace said softly.

Jim's head shot up. "You don't understand," he said in a harsh tone. It was a huge contrast to his normally gentle and happy voice. "When my mother died, she requested that someone find her sheriff son, and don't ask me how she knew I was a sheriff. But she wanted me to become her children's guardian. This is the only thing that she ever asked me to do in my entire life, I need to do it."

"We can still get married, and we can care for them together. I don't mind living with your half siblings," Grace said calmly.

"You don't get it," he said again. "These aren't your normal church kids. It says here..." and he opened up the file of the oldest one, "that their father is in jail, this particular boy has been in trouble with the law. He used to be a drug addict, and he just quit smoking. If I take these people into my home, I can't guarantee that I would feel safe letting you be in the same house."

"Jim, they're your family," she said gently.

"That may be, but between the four of them, we have every problem you can ask for. I could never ask a woman that I loved to go through this with me. This is something that

I'll need to deal with myself." Jim slammed the file shut, and his hands were trembling something awful.

While Grace pleaded with Jim, I flipped through the files. The oldest three were an interesting bunch. The oldest three were half African-American. The oldest and youngest were boys, and the middle one was a girl. I scanned her file. She has some kind of a lung disease that they think is fatal eventually. I shook my head. Jim would have his hands full. The oldest boy had been in trouble with the law before, and the youngest one was allergic to wheat.

I flipped open the folder of the fourth child, a girl of my age, and I nearly jumped out of my chair.

"Jim! This is Jennie!" I said pointing to her picture.

"No it isn't, Jennie's last name is Kerji, not Konley." Jim's voice was irritated. He was almost snapping at me.

"But no, Jim, you know that Jennie has been in that foster home for a little while now and since she didn't know her own name, she just went by theirs."

"We need to go," Grace said walking from the room without a second glance back at Jim. I noticed that she deliberately left the dozen red roses.

I started to follow Grace, I stopped and turned around to say one last thing to Jim, but he had his face in his hands, and his shoulders were shaking. I think he was crying. When I got to the car, Grace was sitting in the driver's seat sobbing. I wanted to scream. Couldn't they just work it out?

# CHAPTER 10
## GONE! 🚓

"Luke is gone," Dad said the moment I entered the house.

"Gone?" I asked. "What do you mean?"

"Just what I said, he's gone. He went for his first meeting with his parole officer, and he didn't come back. He was supposed to be home two hours ago, and he hasn't shown up yet."

"Isn't it a little bit early to be panicking? I mean if he has only been gone for two hours…"

"It's worse than that, Amy." Dad cut me off. "He was seen at the hotel in a brand new car picking up a lady and driving west. There isn't anything west until you get to Washington. If he doesn't get back in time for his meeting next week with the parole officer, he will be in serious trouble, and worse than that, we e-mailed his wife and son plane tickets to come up here this weekend. If they come and Luke isn't here, and if his wife finds out that he drove off in a car with some other lady, she'll never believe him again."

"Surely you trust Uncle Luke more than that," I said. "He's on the straight and narrow road now. He isn't going to leave, because he's trying to serve God."

"I want to believe that he is innocent, I really do, but if he doesn't show up before this weekend with some good explanations, I'll have no choice but to assume the worst," Dad said sadly.

"Have you talked to Jim?" I asked.

"I tried to, but he doesn't seem at all concerned about Luke, he just said that Luke will turn up, and then he hung up, he seemed very preoccupied."

"I know why," I said slowly, and then I told him about what had happened at Jim's office. Dad and Mom went upstairs to talk to Grace, and I found myself standing in the hall by myself.

"What are you doing?" Philip asked coming up behind me.

"I'm not doing much," I said rolling a strand of hair between my fingers. "I don't know how much you know, but we need to pray for both Uncle Luke, and for Grace and Jim."

Philip's blue eyes widened behind his thick glasses, and his dark eyebrows reached for his hairline. "What's wrong with them?"

"They just need prayer," I said simply. Philip led the way into the living room, and we prayed together. I know that God is always there, but something about actually talking to God makes me feel so close to him, and I once more quoted my verse.

"Thou wilt keep him in perfect peace whose mind is stayed on Thee because he trusteth in Thee."

I was going to trust in God no matter what, I resolved. I had trusted Him before, what was to stop me from trusting Him now? Yet somehow, I felt uneasy.

I needed to think, so I hurried down to the bench by the river. As I sat staring at the river, even the shadows seemed to look darker than normal. The sun was still shining, but for some reason, I couldn't shake the feeling that something was wrong.

*Could Jim and Grace be making me feel this way?* I wondered. *Or is it Uncle Luke?*

That grieved me more than anything. If Uncle Luke left now, he would go back to jail, and his wife would never trust him again. I couldn't imagine how hard that was going to be for his son. I didn't even want to be involved in such a mess, but I was. In the midst of all of these crazy things, I had to come around and tell everyone that I had a rib with some hidden something or other that every crook wanted.

*How can I truly trust God when my whole life is in shambles?* My thoughts turned to prayer as I looked up through the trees. *God, what are You doing? I want to trust You, but how can I when You keep messing my life up? I just want to trust You. Please God, help me trust You?* I sighed. Why was this so complicated?

I shut my eyes, and tried to remember the things God had done in my life, but all I could remember was the pain. I could still hear Uncle Keith's fatal words. *I'm not your father.* I could still remember those awful months in the hospital. Even my thoughts of the river in front of me were bitter.

Life could never be that bad again could it? At least not since I was back with the Penners. They were Christians, and they cared about me, they were going to take care of me, weren't they?

"Amy!"

I jumped to my feet and whirled around. No one was there.

"Amy!" This time I knew where the voice was coming from, and I ran for the house. Mom was standing on the porch with a letter in her hand.

"This came for you in the mail today."

I snatched the letter from my mom's hand, and ripped it open. Maybe life could get worse.

*Kid,*

*I know who you are, I know about your precious rib. Don't ever turn your back, I'm always right behind you, and I will get your rib.*

*The Surgeon*

I inhaled sharply, and involuntarily glanced over my shoulder. I could hardly catch my breath. Somewhere out there was a maniac surgeon just waiting to rip out my rib.

"What's wrong?" Mom asked.

I handed her the letter. Mom scanned the sheet of paper. "I'm sure this is just some kind of a joke," she tried to assure me. Putting her arm around me, she led me to Dad's office.

Mom stood with her arm around me as Dad read the short note. He looked up with a very grim look on his face.

"I wouldn't be too worried if I were you. It's just some kind of a scare tactic. If this Surgeon really could carry out this threat, he already would have. But just to be on the safe side, Amy, I don't want you to leave the house without either me or one of your brothers. I don't want to worry you, but make sure that you stay around us, don't run off by yourself. Understood?"

"Yes, Sir." I nodded, but I couldn't get my hands to stop shaking.

Dad came around the desk and leaned against it.

"Honey, I want you to know that I will protect you with my life. You don't have to be afraid. I'll keep an eye on you, and even when I can't see you, God can always see you, He will keep you safe."

Dad's calm voice was reassuring, but I couldn't shake the uneasy feeling of being watched. Could Dad protect me from this evil man?

"I love you, Amy," Dad said giving me a big hug. It hurt my side more than normal, but I hugged him back. Maybe I would be safe. Maybe.

# CHAPTER 11
# HE DOESN'T CARE? 🚓

Two days had gone by, and I hadn't seen any sign of Uncle Luke. Jim hadn't stopped by at all, and Grace's eyes were often red. She hadn't smiled since her last visit with Jim. I hadn't seen any sign of whoever 'The Surgeon' was, but I was still uneasy.

I walked into the room that I was sharing with Grace, and found her sitting on her bed with her Bible in her hands, her long black hair hung in gentle waves around her face, and her red eyes had a slightly more peaceful look than the last time I had seen her.

She looked up with a gentle smile on her tanned face.

"I'm glad you're here," she said patting the bed next to her. I sat down, and she began. "Amy, you were the only one there when Jim and I had that little argument, and I wanted to apologize."

"It's alright. Under the circumstances I think you did very well," I said.

"That's just it. I don't want to be under the circumstances. I am a daughter of the King of kings. I need to praise God no matter what, and not let every little thing that comes upset me. I just read this verse that I've known all my life. I just don't think that I ever understood it like I do now. It's I Thessalonians 5:18 and it commands us to thank God for everything. Amy, I've been acting miserable these last few days because I haven't been thanking and praising God. With God's help, I want to do what Ephesians says, and be 'Giving thanks always for ALL things.' It will make me happier, and it will make everyone around me happier. So I'm asking you, to remind me every time I start complaining, that I'm supposed to give thanks in everything. Can you do that for me?"

I nodded. "But what does this mean for you and Jim?" I asked twisting my fingers together.

"It means," Grace said taking a deep breath. "That I have written a letter to Jim. I told him that I'm willing to wait until he is ready to continue our relationship. If God really wants us to be together, He will make a way."

Grace looked as calm as could be, but I couldn't believe it. They just had to get married.

"Grace, you can't do that, you and Jim need to marry. You are committed to each other, that commitment must never be broken," I said.

"I know, but Jim has a lot going on right now, and I don't think that he is ready to support a family yet. He needs to work out some things first. I will wait for him, but if he doesn't ever come to the place where he's ready, that's alright, it's in God's hands."

"But Grace…"

"Not now, Amy. I just wanted to apologize to you, for my attitude the other day, and for my sulking. The Bible says that we are supposed to rejoice all the time, and so I'm going to rejoice. Now, if you will excuse me, I need to go send this letter to Jim." Grace got up and left the room, and I sat there in silence. Something had to be done.

I ran downstairs grabbed the phone, and dialed Jim's number.

"Hello, Sheriff Trams speaking."

"Hey Jim, this is Amy."

"I'm sorry, Amy, but I'm really busy on a case right now. Could this wait?"

My mind was reeling, he was on a case.

"Have you found out where Uncle Luke is?"

"That's none of my business. He can do what he wants, and if he runs away, I will have no choice but to post a warrant for him. He's not my concern."

"But Jim, he's practically your uncle! Don't you care what happens to him? Can't you help us look for him?"

"What was the point of this call?"

"Grace."

The other end of the line got really quiet, and I wondered if he was still there, finally he spoke.

"Did she ask you to give me a message?"

"No, but you need to do something quick. She doesn't think that you love her. She doesn't think that you really care if you ever marry. Please do something."

"Look, I've got to go." The line went dead, and I wondered why he didn't care. He had always paid attention to our problems before. What was different now? I had just put the phone back when it rang again.

"Hello, this is Amy," I answered.

"Are you one of John's kids?" a woman's voice said. I couldn't decide whether the voice sounded mad, or scared.

"Yes, I am."

"Is your Uncle Luke staying there with you?"

"Yes. But he isn't available right now," I said.

"That's fine. Just tell him that we got the tickets, and that Travis and a friend are going to fly out there. They will be there on Friday at two o' clock at the airport in Rifton on flight one-forty-three. Tell him that he had better be there to get the boys, or else I will write up the divorce papers as fast as I can. Make sure he knows that the boys will be there Friday at two o'clock. Got it?"

"Yes, ma'am."

"Good, and make sure he knows that this is his last chance."

When I hung up, I felt guilty. Why hadn't I told her that her husband was missing? But worst of all where was Uncle Luke? Friday was just two days away, and if he didn't show up by then, his chances of getting back together with his wife were almost none.

I went to Dad's office, and timidly knocked.

"Come in," came Dad's voice. It sounded strained and very busy. "What can I do for you?" he said looking up. That was one thing I loved about Dad, he always looks at you when you're talking to him. I clasped my hands behind my back and began.

"That was Aunt Susanna on the phone."

"Did you tell her Luke isn't here?"

"No," I said looking down. "She said that she's sending Travis and one of his friends, and they are going to be here

Friday at two o'clock, and someone needs to be there to pick them up."

Dad sighed. He leaned back and drummed his fingers on the desk. "I don't know how to tell Susanna this, but I'm afraid that Luke is gone for good. I wanted to think that he was doing well, but now, it must have just been a plot to get out of jail easy. He isn't coming back."

I grabbed a chair and sat down, ignoring the splintering pain in my side. "Dad, I really believe that Uncle Luke got saved. I believe he is trying to do what is right. I don't know where he is, or why he isn't here. But I know that it means the world to him to be here when his son is here. Something is keeping him, and I really think that he is in danger. Uncle Luke would be here if he could, he is a Christian."

"Amy, I don't know where Luke is, but he must be doing something wrong or he would be here. The facts all point to something wrong. I'm afraid I'll have to call Susanna back and tell her not to bother sending the boys."

"Can't we please wait? Uncle Luke might be coming back."

"It's not that simple, Amy. Friday is only two days away."

"I have a plan," I said letting out my breath.

Dad paused and stared at me for a few seconds. "Start talking."

"We don't know if Uncle Luke is being kept away because of something or someone, or if he may even be held captive somewhere. If you were in his shoes, and something was detaining you, wouldn't you want him to believe to the last that you were innocent? We don't really know that he is doing anything wrong, he may just be being detained somehow."

"It doesn't matter if he's innocent. If he isn't back by his parole date, he's in trouble and he knows it. Susanna needs to be told that he's missing."

"Dad, if I was Uncle Luke's daughter, and he didn't come back, I would want to wait till the very last minute to jump to any conclusions. Can't we please wait to tell them?"

"If you wait too long, then they'll fly out here for nothing. I want to believe that Luke is living right, but he has left me no choice but to assume the worst."

"That's where my plan comes in. I don't want us to tell them till the last minute. And we don't have to."

"I'm not sure that I follow you, Amy. If they show up at the airport, and Luke isn't there, it is doubtful that Susanna will ever speak to him again. Or us for that matter."

"Yes, but it's been several years since Travis saw his dad, so if YOU were to pick him up, he wouldn't have any clue that you weren't his real dad."

Dad stared at me. "You're asking me to impersonate my brother? Absolutely not," he said shaking his head. "It's out of the question."

"You wouldn't really be impersonating him. I mean you look like him already. If you met Travis at the airport, than we could have a little extra time to find Uncle Luke."

"Amy, we can't make Luke come back. Luke left of his own accord, and I don't think he's coming back. As much as I want to believe that he changed, it just doesn't look that way."

"But what if Uncle Luke is being kept away? What if he is hurt, or maybe even kidnapped?"

"Kidnapped?" Dad raised an eyebrow. "I think maybe you've got too big of an imagination."

I bit my lip. Why couldn't I ever say anything right?

Dad sighed. "If you can give me any evidence that he is being kept away forcefully before tomorrow, then I will not call Susanna, and I will meet the boys at the airport. But I will not, I repeat, I will not pretend to be my brother. I don't want to play with Travis's emotions."

"Thanks, Dad." I lowered my head in shame. I really did sound silly.

Dad set his pen on the desk and pushed his chair back. "Come here, Amy."

I timidly walked around the desk. Staring at my feet, I bit my lip again. Dad opened his arms, and I walked into them. As I squeezed Dad, tears came to my eyes. Some of it was from the pain in my ribs, but there was something more. Would I always be able to hug him like this? Would we always be together? Would I always have a Dad to love me?

I left the room with only one thing to worry about. I had to prove that Uncle Luke was being held against his will. Jim wasn't going to be any help, so I knew it was up to me. With a determined mind, I set off for the guest room where Uncle Luke had stayed the night before he left.

I couldn't see any changes. Uncle Luke didn't really have anything there. Apparently since he had been moving around so much, he had gotten rid of everything except the necessities. And then when he had come up here, and gotten arrested, he had lost the few belongings that he had.

On the floor at the foot of the bed was the outfit that he had been wearing when he got out of jail, which meant that he was wearing the outfit that Dad had bought him. It looked to me like he had just walked out of the room, and hadn't returned yet.

I stood in the middle of the floor, and looked around. Dad had said that the last spot he had been seen was at the hotel in town, so maybe that was my best option.

I hurried outside and found Paul.

"Hey, Paul, can you take me to town?"

Paul didn't even look up, he just shook his head. He was leaning over the engine of an old pickup truck. The hood was propped up with a stick, and Paul's greasy hands were twisting some piece of the engine.

"It's really important," I pleaded.

Paul just shook his head again.

"You don't have a stutter any more, and you are allowed to talk," I said.

This time Paul looked up. "I'm sorry, but I don't have time," he said, and then he turned back to his work.

I found the same story when I asked Timothy and Grace. Samuel told me he would love to take me, but that it wasn't legal because he only had a farm driving permit. Philip told me to just ask Dad, but I knew Dad was busy too. So I sat down at the kitchen table in despair. If I didn't find out something definite today, then Dad would have to call Aunt Susanna, and Uncle Luke would never see his family again.

*If I could only get Jim to help me*, I thought. Jim had been very distant since he had told Grace that he couldn't marry her. In fact, he had been a complete hermit.

Then Grace's words came back to me. *'I want to do what Ephesians says, and be giving thanks always for all things.'* Was I complaining? Was I supposed to be giving thanks that things weren't working out? I bit my lip. If Grace could rejoice and give thanks when she and Jim were having complications, than I could be thankful that no one would take me to town. *Thank You, God,* I prayed silently.

"Amy?" a voice called. It wasn't a voice that I heard very often, but I knew that it was Paul's.

# CHAPTER 12
# THE WRONG EVIDENCE 🚓

Sitting with Paul in the car wasn't as awkward as it had once been. I had learned to appreciate his silence. He went in stretches where he would talk and stretches where he wouldn't. This was one of his stretches where he wasn't talking. He didn't say a word the entire way to town.

When we got to town, he pulled into the hotel parking lot and stopped. I just stared at him.

"Go on," he said.

"When will you be back?"

Paul looked at his watch, and shrugged. So I got out of the car and headed for the hotel lobby. The Larson's Roost was run by an elderly Swedish couple who prided themselves in the fact that they have the most respectable hotel in town. It was the only hotel in town.

I walked into the lobby, and was greeted by Mrs. Larson.

"Why, Amy! I heard that you were just reunited with your family. I'm so happy for you."

"Thank you, Mrs. Larson."

"What can I do for you child? Yer not lookin at getting a room so that you don't have to stay with yer family are you?" she asked with a smile.

"No, Ma'am, I'm here to ask about my Uncle Luke. I understand that you were the last one to see him."

The smile left Mrs. Larson's face.

"Ya, sure, I vas indeed. But I wish I had never seen that despicable man in my life. He is a disgrace to our community. And to think that he is so ungrateful as to throw Pastor Penner's gift of freedom back in his face." She shook her head. "I hope that I never have to see him again. He is a shame to your good family name. To think that he would run off with another woman when he still has a wife..."

"What exactly did you see?" I asked interrupting her narrative on why she didn't like my uncle. "You didn't see him actually do anything wrong did you?"

"You betcha I did. I was sitting right here, when he walked in. 'Good mornin, Pastor,' I said, and 'e ignored me. I was rather upset at his attitude, and I was about to tell 'im off when a woman came down the stairs. She weren't very pretty, but she was carrying a suitcase. I remembered her from the night before, she came in here, and asked for a room at about eleven o'clock. She said her name was Miss Mikayla Johnson. Of course I didn't believe 'er, she had a look about 'er that I didn't like. But she showed me identification, and I had to give 'er a room."

"What did she look like?" I asked.

"She was average height, middle age, and rather strong looking for a woman. She wore a business suit, and she walked like she was a strutting peacock." Mrs. Larson tapped her pen against her chin.

"Go on," I said.

"When she came down the stairs, Luke took 'er bag, and brought 'er to the car. He got the door for 'er, and then got into this fancy black car. I think it was new. They both looked guilty the whole time. He looked like a cat had his tongue, and she acted like they was being watched. I didn't like the whole scenario. Seeing as I thought it was Pastor Penner and all, I was very upset. So I called your home, and Pastor Penner answered, so I knew that it had to be his twin brother. And like I said, I hope I never see that scoundrel again."

"What if he turned out to be innocent?" I asked, "Maybe it was something else? Maybe you didn't understand what you saw?"

"Trust me child, I know what I saw. Men don't get the door for their colleague like that. Men get the door only for their sweetheart. Or if they are really polite, but I don't think Luke is that polite."

I opened my mouth to argue. I thought Uncle Luke was very polite, but instead I bit my lip. I wasn't supposed to argue and complain, I was supposed to give thanks.

"Thank you for your help," I said turning to leave.

"Ya, sure. You betcha, any time."

When I got outside, there was no sign of Paul, so I decided to walk to Jim's office. It wasn't very far away, and I knew that Paul would be able to figure out where I was.

As I entered his office, Miss Jensen was leaving. Jim looked grim but firmly determined. When he saw me, he scowled.

"I take it you just told her that you're going to become your siblings guardian?"

"What do you want?" Jim asked ignoring my question.

"Grace would be willing to live with your siblings and their problems. Besides, if Jennie is coming as well, she won't be a problem."

"Jennie is coming," he said. "They're all coming and you can't talk me out of it."

I couldn't help but smile.

"I haven't seen Jennie for so long," I said. "She was the best and only friend I had. I'm so glad that you're bringing her up here."

Jim took a deep breath. "I'm a very busy man, and I don't have time to just chat. What do you want?"

I sat down across from his desk, and decided that if he wanted me to get to the point then I was going to do just that.

"I came here, because Uncle Luke was seen leaving the hotel with a woman in a new car. We know that he couldn't afford a new car, and he was supposed to be here this weekend when his son came. If he isn't here when his son gets here, he will never be able to get back together with Aunt Susanna. If he isn't back soon, he will miss his parole date, and then he will go back to jail. I need your help to get him back."

Jim leaned forward. "Travis is coming this weekend?"

I nodded. A strange look crossed Jim's face. Shrugging he leaned back. "It can't be helped."

"What can't?" I asked.

Jim started drumming his fingers on the desk in an uncharacteristic manner. "Are you done yet?"

"Yes," I said waiting for him to tell me what to do.

"Well, it's not my problem if your uncle decides to divorce. If he wants to marry someone else it's not my concern. If he isn't back for the parole meeting, than it will be my job to arrest him, but until then, he is none of my concern. Now may I ask you to leave? I have a lot of work to do."

I rose wordlessly and left his office, Jim seemed so different somehow. He had always wanted to help us, what had changed? Yet somehow, I got the impression that he knew more than he was saying.

I stopped at the front desk and leaned my elbows on the high counter. When a shoot of pain came from my ribs I lowered them. "Excuse me, but can I ask you a few questions?" I asked the secretary.

"Sure, go ahead."

"Have you noticed any change in the sheriff's attitude? He seems different," I asked.

She shrugged. "He's always had times when he looks sick and tired, and over worked, but I would agree with you that there is something wrong. He's not as pleasant as he used to be."

"Do you have any idea what it could be?" I asked.

"No." She paused. "He's been this way ever since the day that he told Grace he couldn't marry her, so maybe it's the responsibility of being in charge of these kids. But then I've never known responsibility to bother him." Tapping her pen against the desk she thought for a moment. Finally she leaned forward. "He's been a lot quieter lately, and I think he might be working on something." She lowered her voice. "I may be wrong, but if I know anything, he acts like he is afraid of something. I can't imagine him being afraid of anything, but that's how he's acting."

"Well thank you for talking to me," I said.

"You know Jim is almost like a son to me, and I don't like seeing him upset. If you can think of anything to cheer him up, let me know. I tried to talk about Grace with him, because I thought maybe that would cheer him up, but he said he doubted he would live long enough to marry her."

My head jerked up at that. "What do you mean he doesn't think he'll live that long?"

"Well, like I said, he seems scared of something. He's been very jumpy even at the slightest noises."

"Thank you," I said as I turned to go, but Jim stopped me.

"Can you give this to your dad?" He held out an envelope. I could hardly look at the envelope. All I could see was Jim's face. Beads of sweat lined his forehead, and it wasn't from heat. His cheeks were a greyish color and his features twisted into a look of pain. If he hadn't been in his uniform, I would have thought that he belonged in a hospital he looked so bad.

I reached out and took the envelope.

"Sure, I'll give it to Dad. Hey, why don't you come over to supper tonight? You look like you could use a break."

Jim shook his head so violently that I thought his neck might snap. His voice trembled.

"I can't put your family in danger, I love you all too much for that. Just give that envelope to Uncle John, and tell him that I'll miss him."

"Are you going somewhere?" I asked.

Jim looked around like he was being watched.

"I hope not. But I don't know if I'll survive long enough to see him again. I'm in the middle of something very serious. I can't tell you what, but I probably won't live through it. Tell

Grace I'm sorry. I really want to be her husband, but if I married her now, she would be a widow next week. I couldn't wish that upon someone that I love as much as I love her. Good-bye Amy." He turned and walked back to his office.

I followed him to his office, and walked in without knocking. He was sitting in his chair with his head in his hands. I walked over and put my hand on his shoulder, he jerked up so fast that it made me jump. In his hand was a gun.

When he saw that it was me, he holstered it.

"Don't sneak up on me like that, you might get shot." Jim was actually trembling.

"Can't you get help?" I asked.

"From who? I am the Law." He looked around frantically again. "You need to leave. It's not safe for you here."

"Maybe Dad can help?" I asked.

"No. You need to go right now." His commanding voice couldn't be refused, so I left. Paul was waiting for me in the lobby.

"How did you know I was here?" I asked when we got to the car.

Paul shrugged.

"I think Jim needs help," I said. Paul shrugged again. In the middle front seat, I saw a box with some sort of a mechanical part in it, there was also a few bags of groceries in the back seat.

When we got home, Paul took the mechanical part, and went back to the truck that he was working on. I took the groceries to the house.

"Did you find out anything?" Dad asked when I walked in the kitchen.

"No. But Dad, I really believe that Uncle Luke is innocent. I know it looks bad for him, but I believe with all my heart that something is wrong or he would be here. It means the world to him that he sees his son, he wouldn't stay away on his own accord," I pleaded. Dad crossed his arms and looked away. There was pain in his eyes.

"You know Amy, I agree with you. We can only find the wrong evidence, but I want to believe Luke is right. So, I'm going to wait to tell Susanna. If he isn't here when Travis gets here, then we will tell them, but I want to give Luke extra time to prove that he's innocent. I'm not quite ready to admit that he is going back to his old ways."

"Thank you, Dad," I said. Reaching into my purse I pulled out the envelope. "Jim gave me this to give to you."

Dad opened the envelope and scanned the paper, as he read, his brow furrowed, and the corners of his mouth turned down.

"What is it?" I asked.

"We need to have a family meeting," Dad said heading upstairs.

# CHAPTER 13
# SCARED 🚓

We all sat in complete silence as Dad read us the letter. It wasn't quite a suicide note, but it was the closest to one I had ever heard.

*Dear Pastor John,*

*You've been like an uncle to me, and I've always thought of you as a friend, someone that I can trust with my deepest secrets and worries. I'll never forget all the conversations we have had. And the time that I asked you for Grace. I want nothing more than to have her, but I'm not going to live long enough to marry her. Please tell her that I still love her, and wish it didn't have to be like this. It pains me to think of her at anyone else's side. But if you find a man that is worthy of her, please don't let her remain single because of me. I love you all more than my own family, and I don't want to have to tell you this, but I want you to sing "Stars in my Crown" at my funeral, I won't hear of anyone else doing my funeral. Make sure you share the gospel clearly since I know some of the men that will be there aren't saved. You're probably wondering why I'm telling you all of this. Well I can't tell you why. If I told you, you would be in danger as well. I don't want to put you through the pain of trying to stay alive. Just trust me. I fight for freedom. Don't let Grace grieve as much as I grieve, or she will never smile again. My heart is broken but I can't ask her to go through this with me. By the time you get this, I will be on my way to certain death. No, I'm not throwing away my life for nothing. I intend to bring him down with me. You don't know who 'he' is, and I can't tell you, but if I take him out, it will save hundreds of lives. Know that I die with honor.*

*With fond memories of our past,*
*Jim Trams*

Dad looked up. "Does anyone have any idea what he means?"

I looked around the room, Grace had tears streaming down her cheeks, and everyone else had very solemn looks on their faces.

"I think I have an idea," Paul said.

Dad looked up and gave Paul an encouraging nod.

"When we were in town, I noticed a guy standing outside of the police station. I wouldn't have noticed him, but he was hiding behind a dumpster, and I tend to notice hiding people. I wouldn't have thought that much about him if it weren't for the fact that he looked a lot like Jim, only twenty years older. I think Jim's dad might be in town."

"He's in jail for killing an officer," I said.

"Not any more, there was a jail break two weeks ago, down in Los Angeles, and he got out." Paul seemed to know everything, but no one bothered asking him how he knew.

"Okay," Dad said. "But why would he be here? What does he have to do with Jim dying?"

Silence reigned in the room. No one had an answer.

Dad sighed. "I'll call Jim's adopted Dad, but he won't know more than this. We can't exactly call the police, since he is the police. All we can do is pray." With that he bowed his head.

"Dear Father, we don't know what is going on with Jim. We ask you to protect him, and bring him back to us. And please Father God, help us know how we can help him. I also want to pray for Luke, please bring him back. In Jesus' precious name, Amen."

We all looked up, and Dad went for the phone, he called Jim's office first, and found that he had left fifteen minutes before in his police car by himself, and he was heading west. He hadn't left any destination with his secretary.

Next Dad called Jim's dad, he knew about as much as we did, and he was very upset. No one seemed to know anything about whatever problem Jim was facing. Dad had just set the phone down when it rang.

"Hello?" Dad answered. "Luke, where are you?" Dad paused again. "Luke? Luke? He hung up."

"What did he say?" I asked.

"He was talking really fast, he said he wasn't supposed to call, but he had to. He just asked me to meet Travis at the airport and to keep him here until he comes back. He said not to tell anyone that he called. I may not be the best judge, but I think he was scared."

I put my head in my hands, everyone seemed scared. What was wrong with everyone? Then I remembered my rib and that awful note from 'The Surgeon'. I was scared too.

The family meeting broke up and the guys went back to work. I couldn't stand all of this, why couldn't my life just be normal?

I knew I wasn't supposed to be afraid, like my verse said, God keeps those in perfect peace, whose minds are stayed on Him. I just needed to keep my mind stayed on Christ and what He did for me on the cross.

I went to my room, and sat down on my mattress. I opened my Bible randomly, and started reading in First Thessalonians chapter five. When I got to verse eighteen, I stopped and read it over.

"In everything give thanks for this is the will of God in Christ Jesus concerning you."

I shook my head. Did that really mean in EVERYTHING? Was I honestly supposed to thank God for my past? Was I supposed to thank God for all of the danger we were facing?

I read it again, "In EVERYTHING give thanks, for this IS the will of God in Christ Jesus concerning you."

*Is this really God's will for my life?* I wondered. *To give thanks?* Could I honestly thank God for everything?

*God? Please help me?* I prayed silently. *I want to trust You in everything, and to give thanks, but I need Your help. Please help me.*

"Amy!" Dad called. I ran downstairs. Dad stood in the hallway at the bottom of the stairs with a pistol in his hands.

"Do you know how to use this?" he asked holding it out to me.

"No," I said not reaching out to take it. The last time I had held a gun, wasn't something that I wanted to remember.

"Well, you're going to learn." Dad had a firm look on his face, and I could tell there was no arguing. "Follow me," he said taking me out back behind the house. "Grace and Mom both know how to use a gun, and I want you to be able to as well."

"Why?" I asked.

"Because I want you to be able to defend yourself when I'm not here," he paused then said, "I'm going to try to find Jim. He needs help, and I'm going to try to help him."

Dad spent the next twenty minutes teaching me how to use the gun. When he was done he went back into the house and gathered the family together again.

"I'm going to help Jim. Timothy, I want you and Paul with me. Samuel, you and Philip take care of the farm and the ladies."

I stared at Dad's tall figure as he talked. His blond hair with its slight sideburns gave his slightly square jaw an even fiercer appearance. He glanced down at me with his blue eyes and gave a slight smile. It softened his face immediately.

"Did you have something you wanted to say, Amy?"

"No, Sir," I said smiling at him.

"Then let's go, men." He turned and ran up the stairs two at a time.

After a few hectic moments the guys left loaded down with everything they could possibly need to survive. They were prepared for anything.

When they finally came back, Dad looked defeated and discouraged. They hadn't found Jim, or any sign of him at all.

When Friday afternoon came, Dad silently left the house to go get Travis and his friend. I had never seen him so discouraged.

When Dad pulled up, I eagerly watched from the window. What would my cousin be like? A tall blondish kid jumped out of the front seat, and ran to the trunk that Dad had popped.

Besides the blond hair, there was no resemblance. His face was oval, with none of the sharp features that Uncle Luke had. I strained to see the other kid in the car, but the porch railing was in the way.

The boy that I assumed was Travis pulled a wheelchair from the car trunk, and unfolded it. Opening the back door of the car, he helped another boy out of the car, and into the wheelchair.

I stepped outside to see if they needed any help carrying bags. When Dad looked up and saw me, his face broke into a smile. "Meet Mike and Travis," Dad said with a hand on each boys shoulder.

"I'm Mike," the taller blond haired boy said. "And that's Travis." He gestured towards the dark haired boy in the wheel chair. "You'll have to excuse him, he had an accident, and he isn't right in the head any more, that's why I'm here to take care of him."

I looked at Travis, and sure enough, his eyes didn't seem to look at anything in particular, his mouth hung open, and his hands were twisted in a funny fashion. His legs were crossed in a scissor-like fashion and he didn't seem to hear any of us. He gurgled something, but I couldn't understand it.

Dad and Mike lifted Travis's wheelchair up the porch steps, and gently set it on the porch. Dad pushed Travis inside, and showed the boys to a room.

I went to the kitchen and got a glass of water. As I stood there drinking it, Dad came in.

"I had no idea that Travis was like that," Dad said. "But this way, he won't know that Luke isn't here yet. I just can't believe Susanna didn't say something. But then maybe it was all part of her plan to see if Luke really has changed. I told Mike that Luke isn't here, but he didn't seem too disturbed, he said they would wait."

"Where could Uncle Luke be?" I asked.

"Search me. Your guess is as good as mine," Dad said shrugging.

"Both Luke and Jim disappeared within a week of each other. Do you think maybe there disappearances are connected?" I asked.

"It's possible, but doubtful. I'm beginning to think that Luke isn't coming back, and as for Jim, we looked in every logical place and couldn't find him. I trust Jim's judgment, and if he needed help, I think he would get it at the office. We just need to trust his judgment. Now, I really need to finish working on my sermon, would you mind trying to make Mike and Travis feel at home? I mean just until the boys come in."

"Sure, Dad," I said and he left.

As I walked towards the boy's bedroom, I thought I heard voices, but when I knocked on the door they stopped.

Mike cracked the door open. "Yeah?" he asked.

"Supper won't be for a while, so do you guys want to look around the farm, or do you want to rest?" I asked.

Mike looked over his shoulder. "We don't really care. I think Travis would like to see his dad's house if that's possible." Mike held the door open a bit wider, and I caught another glimpse of my cousin.

His eyes were rolling around in the sockets, and his mouth hung open, I wondered if he could see anything. He was drooling and mumbling, and his fingers had an odd twist to them.

"Uncle Luke doesn't actually have a place here. He was staying with us. He said that he wasn't going to get a house until he knew where Aunt Susanna wanted to live."

"Oh, well why don't you come in and tell Travis about his dad?" Mike said opening the door all the way. "He hasn't seen him in a long time."

"Do you think he can understand me?" I asked in a whisper.

"No. Not really, but he seems calmer when people talk to him, so I like to talk to him and tell him what's going on."

"What happened to him?" I asked stepping into the room.

Mike shrugged. "Now about his dad?"

"Oh, yes." I sat down on a chair facing Travis' wheelchair and started. "Your dad looks just like my dad, and he sounds the same too. He is kind and strong, and he seems very thoughtful."

"Amy, you sound like you're talking to a wall. Travis may not be normal in your eyes, but try to talk to him like he is. Look him in the eye, and be friendly, he isn't a baby you know."

I was a little bit shocked at Mike's speech, so when I started, I pretended like I was talking to Mike, only I was looking at Travis.

"Uncle Luke used to scare me, he used to be a very hard man, but when he became a Christian, he changed. Now he is kind, gentle, and he wants to make things right. He loves God with all of his heart, and he wants to be an honorable man. You'll like him a lot. I think he's great."

"A Christian you say?" Mike asked arching an eyebrow.

"Yes, he's changed a lot."

"I'm sure. He's like the rest of those Christians I suppose. He probably thinks that we are all sinners going to Hell, but because Jesus died on the cross for him and he repented that he is going to Heaven." Mike snorted. "Hallelujah!" he mocked.

"Yes. He does believe that, because it's true." I defended.

"Right. And I'm sure he is just happy as a squirrel that he is forgiven and going to Heaven. Maybe he prefers the company of the angels to that of his son." Mike's mocking voice grated on me and I wanted to snap back, instead I bit my lip. I just needed to be thankful for Mike.

"It's true Mike, we are all sinners and need Jesus to forgive us." I tried not to sound as upset as I really was.

"Yeah sure, whatever. Now back to Luke. Tell Travis about him."

"I think I've told just about everything I know."

"Where is he now?" Mike asked, and I couldn't help but cringe under his sneering gaze. "Maybe he's at the church confessing his sins to God?"

I ignored his crude comments and answered as best I could. "I don't know where he is. He was last seen several days ago at the hotel."

"I thought he was staying here? Why isn't he back yet?" Mike's questions were more nosey than necessary. He acted like he was trying to find out what he could so he could tell Aunt Susanna that Uncle Luke wasn't any good.

I figured I wasn't doing any good keeping it a secret, so I told exactly what had been seen.

"So, Travis's old man ran off with another lady. That'll go over great with Susanna," Mike said.

"I don't really think that he left on his own accord," I said, ignoring Mike's disrespectful tone.

"What do you mean? It sure seems to me like he did."

"I know it seems that way, but I know that it meant the world to Uncle Luke to see Travis again. That's all he talked about that first day. He really feels bad about the past, and he really wanted to be here when Travis was. He would be here if he could be."

"Really?" There was doubt in his voice. "Well where do you think he is?"

"I don't know, but he could be being held captive somewhere. Maybe someone threated to hurt Travis if he didn't go with them. I don't know, but I know that I trust him and I don't think he just left."

Travis was gurgling more than normal and his hands were flying in twisted patterns. Apparently my talking to him hadn't calmed him down at all. Maybe he did understand and it upset him.

"What can we do to help?" Mike asked. I gave him a blank look so he continued. "I mean if Luke really was kidnapped, or something, how can we help get him back and prove that he's innocent? I'm not saying I think he is, in fact I don't think that he is innocent, but if he is, how do we help him?"

"The only man I know of that could help us just disappeared," I mumbled. We needed Jim.

"Can't we call the police or something? I mean isn't Luke going to be in trouble anyway for not making his parole meeting?"

"That's the problem," I said. "The sheriff disappeared."

"I'm sure the sheriff isn't the only law around here."

I snapped my fingers. "Officer Tony!" I said jumping to my feet. "He could help, and he's a Christian too," I said smiling.

"Oh, so now you have to be a Christian to be helpful," Mike snorted.

"I'm not saying that," I bit my lip. *There goes my tongue again getting into trouble.* "It's just that because he has asked God to forgive his sins, he tries to live the way God wants him to."

"Right, that makes him better than the rest of us normal people."

I bit my lip again, I wanted more than anything to argue back, but I didn't think that it was right. Jesus didn't even open His mouth when He was being questioned before His death. If he could keep quiet, then I would try. It wasn't going to make Mike believe in Jesus simply because I argued with him, so I kept my mouth shut and headed for the phone.

"What did he say?" Mike asked when I hung up.

"He said that he had a lot going on, but that he was doing some research. He's going to stop by later this afternoon with some information. He seemed just as worried as Jim was when I talked to him."

"Who's Jim?"

"Jim is our sheriff. He seemed really worried about something, and then he left. He was supposed to marry Grace, but something came up, and he said he can't marry her yet."

"Who's Grace?"

"She's my sister."

"Oh. You probably already knew this, but Travis doesn't know anything about his cousins, why don't you tell him about them?"

I thought it was weird how Mike wanted me to tell Travis so much. Travis obviously wasn't paying attention, or interested. But then maybe Mike wanted to know and didn't feel right asking for himself.

I took them to the living room and told them about each of my family members and showed him the picture with each one. Travis seemed to actually be looking at the pictures, but I couldn't tell for sure since his eyes seemed to look everywhere, there was even a few times where his eyes were looking in different directions. And other times his eyes crossed.

That night at supper, Mike cut up Travis' food into tiny pieces and spoon fed him. Something about it all seemed strange. I couldn't imagine any mother sending off her son that was this handicapped by himself on a plane with just a friend.

And what was wrong with Mike? Most boys his age won't even look at someone handicapped, let alone treat them like their best friend. Something was fishy. I just couldn't put my finger on it.

There was a knock on the door. "Amy, would you get that?" Mom asked as she sat down at the table with two pie plates. I jumped up and headed for the door.

"Come in, Officer Tony. We were just ready for dessert. You're welcome to join us."

"No, thank you. I just need to talk to your father."

I led him into the kitchen and got him a chair. He sat down by Dad, and I couldn't help but think of the contrast between him and Jim. Jim acted like he owned the house, Officer Tony acted like he was scared to touch anything.

"Maybe we should discuss this in private?" Officer Tony said when he realized that the whole table was waiting for him to speak.

"If it's not necessary to keep a secret, I would just assume everyone here knows what you have to say," Dad said.

"Well, if you insist," Officer Tony rubbed the back of his neck and began. "Sheriff Trams left me in charge of his office while he's gone. He didn't tell me where he was going, but he left stuff all over his office that gave me clues, and I believe he did it on purpose. He knows he needs our help. The only reason I'm discussing this with you, is because I'm not sure who else to go to for help. When Luke disappeared, I know it looked like we weren't doing anything, but we were. Jim wouldn't speak of it even to me, but I think he might know where Luke is. Anyway, Luke's parole officer has seemed very nervous lately, and from one of the papers I found in

Sheriff Tram's office, I think that the sheriff may have a trap set for him."

"For the parole officer?" Dad asked.

"Yes. The parole officer, from all I can tell, it looks like he might be doing some things he shouldn't. Taking situations like Luke's and telling them that if they pull off this job for him, usually a robbery or something, he'll let them off easy. I remember this happening once before around here where the parole officer was crooked. He always made it look like the ex-cons were the ones in the wrong. Jim seems to be hot on his trail, and he doesn't seem to know about it. It seems to me that the parole officer is still following his plan, because he thinks that Luke is in it with him. What he doesn't know is that Luke is living on the side of the law now, and isn't going to break the law to save his neck. So if I have my facts right, Sheriff Trams was going to spring his trap tomorrow, using Luke as the bait, and catch the parole officer in the wrong. This is the first break we've ever had on him, and, from everything I know, it should work. But the sheriff is gone, and from everything I can find, he is working on another case, a very serious one."

"What kind of serious case?" Grace asked with worry written all over her face.

"I don't know exactly, but it has something to do with a plane being blown up, and it seems to me that he is in extreme danger. The mayor is scheduled to be on flight 703 this afternoon. I think Jim thinks someone is going to try to high-jack it. I don't even think the sheriff knows how much danger he is in. I think we might be dealing with a villain who goes by the name of 'The Surgeon.'"

I jerked my head up at that bit of news.

"I think Jim might have an idea of the danger." Dad pulled the letter from Jim out of his pocket and handed it to Officer Tony.

When Officer Tony looked up, fear was written all over his face.

"The sheriff knew that I would read this. This line about 'I can't tell you who he is' was written for me. He knew that I would know who it was. He is in more danger than I thought. We're all in extreme danger." The look on Officer Tony's face was nothing but fear, and it struck fear into my heart.

# CHAPTER 14
# CAUGHT 🚗

"Amy, you need to come with us," I cringed at Officer Tony's command.

Dad stepped forward. "I don't think that's best. I want her here, where she's safe,"

"Trust me, John, I don't want her getting hurt any more than you do, but since she's involved, I think she needs to come. I don't think it would be safe to leave her here. 'The Surgeon' will find her."

We had shown Officer Tony the threat note that I had received, and it had just agitated him more.

"Why can't we send her to my parents place?" Dad asked again. I looked at Dad's tense face. He was pleading for my safety out of his love for me.

"You don't understand, John. This 'Surgeon' will find her there, it's best that she's with us, he no doubt knows where she is now, and I'm sure that if you left her anywhere he would make his move."

"Who is this 'Surgeon'?" Dad asked, "And why is he so feared?"

"I can't explain it all, but he sent a note very similar to the one that Amy received to Jim. Only it wasn't about a rib, it was about a flight number. Trust me. This guy is not to be messed with. I think I know enough now to know where the sheriff and Luke are, and we need to get to them. I sent some men to the airport to watch that plane, and I sent some men ahead of us to make sure the way is safe. I don't want to bring you into this, but quite frankly I don't know what else to do. You and your sons are all level headed and know how to use a gun. I need your help. I guess you could say I'm deputizing you for the day."

"Where is the rest of your department?" I asked.

"They're all out on other small jobs. The 'Surgeon' knew that, and I think he set them up. For instance, we have two men down at the Manson homestead, keeping an eye on things since we received a warning about that being their hide out. We have been all over the county, and we know that most of them are probably just distractions, but if we leave them, than 'The Surgeon' will go there. He is very smart, now enough time wasted, we need to go."

I didn't really understand what was happening, but I knew that it wasn't good. Dad, Samuel, and I went with Officer Tony and Timothy followed behind in our car with Paul, Philip, Mike and Travis. Mom and Grace took the van and headed for Grandpa Elwood's house.

As we drove to town, my mind filled with hundreds of questions. "Why do we have to leave our home?"

"It's not safe," Officer Tony said. "You just need to trust me."

We stopped at the police station and Officer Tony told Philip, Mike, Travis and I to all stay there. He said it wasn't safe for us to follow them, and it wasn't safe for us to be unprotected, so we went in and sat around the Sheriff's office. I noticed a higher security in the lobby than usual, and it just made me wonder more than ever what was going on.

"What are you doing?" Philip asked me as I pulled open the top drawer on Jim's desk.

"I'm trying to figure out what is going on." I said flipping through a stack of papers.

"That's probably not legal, Amy."

I didn't even look up, "Look at this!" I said grabbing a paper from the bottom of the stack. It was a report of some kind, but what struck me, was the name at the bottom. It was Miss Mckayla Johnson, and next to it, in tiny print, it said 'also known as Officer Wilson'.

"What is that?" Mike asked me.

"This is a paper by the woman who left with Uncle Luke. It looks like..." I paused as I scanned the paper, "It looks like she isn't really Miss Johnson, but Officer Wilson. No wonder Mrs. Larson told me she looked strong."

"You're saying that Travis' dad left with a policewoman?"

I nodded. "Jim must have sent her and told Luke to go with her. He's probably being kept hidden until the trap can be sprung. At least we know he's safe."

I started flipping through another stack of papers.

"Amy, you really ought to stop. I don't think you're supposed to do that," Philip said. I looked up and met his concerned blue eyes. Brothers. Why do they always have to be right? Then my conscious pricked me. *In EVERYTHING give thanks!* It reminded me.

"Well, are we just supposed to sit here until we turn to skeletons?" I asked.

"I think we should pray," Philip said.

"You start," I said bowing my head. Because like always, Philip was right. I silently asked God's forgiveness for not being thankful.

"Dear Father," Philip prayed. "We need help. We don't know what's wrong, or why Jim and Officer Tony are so scared. We don't know what to do. Please give Jim wisdom. Keep Dad and the boys safe, please help us to be patient, please be with them, and help them to have the strength to do what they need to do. Give them courage. In Jesus' precious name I pray, Amen." I prayed when he was done, and when we looked up, my eyes met Mike's scowling ones.

"So, that will make everything better. Now we just wait, and God will work a miracle. Why didn't you ask for some donuts while you were at it, I'm hungry," Mike said with a smirk on his face. I bit my lip again. *In everything give thanks*. Why was this so hard? When I thanked God for everything I was happier, but somehow it was really hard. *God please help me.* I prayed silently. *Help me to be thankful for Mike.*

"That's right Mike," Philip said holding his head high. "Mock all you want, but when you die, don't blame me when you wish that you had paid more attention."

"Oh, right, I forgot, I suppose you think I'm going to burn in Hell forever because I'm a sinner. I suppose if I begged God to forgive my sins, than I could go to Heaven, and be happy all the time." Mike dropped to his knees and pretended to pray. His mocking attitude was really getting to me. And I could hold my tongue no longer.

"Fine. Don't believe that Jesus died and shed His blood for you. Don't believe that there is life after this, and don't believe that God loves you so much that He sent his only Son to die the most horrible death for you. Believe whatever you want, but I can guarantee that within seconds after you die, you will wish that you had listened to us," I pleaded with him.

Mike just smirked. "Whatever."

"Hey look," Philip said pointing out the window into the lobby. In the front door came four police officers. In the middle of them was a man handcuffed and he looked furious. He wore a dress shirt and khaki pants with grass stains on them.

"Who's that?" I asked.

"Someone who broke the law," Mike said with a snort.

I felt like giving a smart reply back, but I knew that it wasn't the right thing to do, so instead I went to the lobby to ask.

"Hey, you're alive," the man in handcuffs said in disbelief.

"Who are you?" one of the officers asked me.

"I'm Amy Penner," I said. He just nodded, and three of the officers took the guy to the back of the building.

"Who was that?" I asked.

"That was Sam Maxin. He used to be a parole officer, but now he's a prisoner," one of the officers told me.

"Was he Luke Penner's parole officer?" I asked.

"Yes, he was. He asked Luke to kidnap you for him, but Luke went straight to Sheriff Trams, and that's how we set the trap for him. Luke has been hiding out until the capture could be made."

I was aware of the fact that Mike had pushed Travis out into the hall and that he had heard all of that, but I didn't think that it would do any good for him to know that his dad was innocent. He didn't understand enough for it to matter to him.

"Where is Uncle Luke?" I asked.

"I don't know. He was with Officer Wilson. She was supposed to take him back here. They should be here by now."

"Maybe you should go find them," I suggested.

"That won't be necessary. The sheriff told us to report to him as soon as we caught Sam. So if you'll excuse me, I'll contact him."

"He isn't here," Philip said.

"I know that son," the officer said as he pushed a button on his little radio.

"Come in Sheriff, this is Officer Lanskey reporting about Sam Maxin." There was a long pause. "Sheriff Trams come in please," he repeated.

"Do you know where the sheriff is?" He asked the secretary.

"No, Sir. I don't, but he left this for you," she said pulling a sealed envelope out from under her desk.

Officer Lanskey tore open the envelope and his eyes scanned the paper. When he was done, his face mirrored the same fear that I had seen in Jim's eyes. He looked up at us.

"Why are you kids here?" he asked.

"Officer Tony said that it would be safest for us here," Philip said.

"Well he was right. I don't want you kids leaving unless you get permission." Officer Lanskey crumpled the note in one hand and shoved it in his pocket. "Men?" he said turning around to the officers behind him. "The sheriff needs help. I think I know where he is, and I'm guessing Officer Wilson is probably already on her way there with or without Luke. We need to be there too."

The men left and I sat down on a chair in the lobby and stared out the window. What was I supposed to do? Everyone seemed to be going to help the sheriff, but I didn't even know where he was. All I wanted was to see Uncle Luke safe and to be home with my family. I leaned forward on my elbows but an intense pain ripped through my ribs and my chest tightened. I bolted back to an upright position. Why did I have to be in pain at a time like this?

"What's wrong, Amy?" Philip asked when he saw me rubbing the tender spot on my side. "You don't look very good."

I wanted to complain, I wanted to be cranky, and I wanted to cry about the pain, but that verse about giving thanks in everything kept going through my mind, if Paul in the Bible could give thanks for his pain than so could I. Besides the Bible didn't say to give thanks when you feel like it. It commands us to be *Giving Thanks always for ALL things*.

"I'll be fine, I just hurt a little." I tried to smile, but it turned into a grimace. He looked very concerned, but I wasn't about to tell him that this was normal. I was used to pain. Ever since before I had had surgery the first time, I had felt pain in my ribs. Some days it was barely noticeable, and other days it was unbearable. I had been in a good stretch for a while where it hadn't hurt much, but it really hurt now.

I sat back, and shut my eyes as I waited for the pain to subside.

"Amy," Philip hissed. He grabbed my hand and pulled me toward Jim's office, I gasped as the pain shot through my side, when we got into the office. Philip pulled me to my knees behind the door. He crouched beside me, and Mike and Travis somehow managed to be there as well.

"What's wrong?" I whispered.

"Someone is coming toward the front door, and he looks like the man Paul described, I don't think Jim wants you to be seen by any cutthroats."

I tried to lean forward to hear what he said to the secretary when he came in, but leaning forward sent another spasm of pain through my ribcage. Biting my lip I tried to control the pain, but tears came to my eyes.

I squirmed under the intense pain in my side, but I also tried to be as quiet as I could, I wanted to hear what was going on.

"Fire! Fire!" someone yelled.

"Where?" One of the security guards asked.

"Right next door at the hotel!"

I tried to get up but Philip laid a hand on my shoulder and shook his head. We waited a few moments, until the excitement in the lobby had died down, and then we got up. The lobby was back to minimum security, and smoke billowed up from the hotel next door.

The smoke reminded me of that awful day that I had nearly burned to death. If Philip hadn't been there, I would have died.

"What if there are people that need help?" I asked thinking of what a help Philip was in situations like this.

"I agree," Philip said. "We should help if we can."

"You kids had better stay here. It's my orders to keep you safe," one of the security guards said.

"Look here, Dude," Mike said stepping forward and sticking his finger in the security guard's face. "There are a lot of people out there, it's not like we're going to be going down a back alley or anything. We'll be right there in the middle of all those people. Perfectly safe," Mike said, and I couldn't help but feel embarrassed by his rudeness.

"Let's go," he said leading the way.

"I suppose it is pretty safe, but be careful," the guard warned us.

"Look, there between the buildings!" Philip said pointing at a fleeing figure that was leaving the hotel. I wouldn't have given him the time of day if it hadn't have been for the fact that he was running away from the crowd.

"Maybe he started the fire," Mike said and he took off after him.

"Wait here, Amy, I don't want you getting hurt, I'm going to stop Mike," Philip said leaving my side and chasing after Mike.

So there I was standing in the middle of a crowd with a handicapped boy in a wheelchair at my side.

"Excuse me, miss," a soft, worried voice said. I turned around and found myself staring at a small woman. She was about my height, and soot clung to her face. She looked very worried.

"Can I help you?" I asked.

"Yes, you see I want to get my stuff to my car, but I can't carry it all, and I don't want to leave it here with all these people hanging about. Would you please help me take it to my car?"

I eyed the woman with caution, she seemed nice enough, and I could clearly see that she wasn't going to be able to carry the three suitcases and the garment bag that she had at her feet.

"Sure," I said reaching down to grab one of the suitcases. The moment I lifted, a hot pain ripped through my side. A small cry escaped my lips as I dropped the bag.

"Are you alright child? I don't want to hurt you," she said.

I looked at the bags, I wasn't going to be able to carry them, but I couldn't leave Travis here alone anyway.

"Here, you can maybe put some of those suitcases across the wheelchair handle bars, and I can push his wheelchair. He won't mind," I said feeling bad for the poor woman.

"Oh, thank you," she said placing a suitcase across the front of Travis' chair. Travis didn't seem to notice that he didn't have any arm rests, or that he had a suitcase and a garment bag pressing against his chest, he just gurgled and drooled like always.

"There, if you can push him, than I will carry these two bags," she said reaching down and picking up the other two. "My car is over there," she said motioning with her head.

We walked away from the sirens and fire trucks toward a small parking lot at the grocery store. My side hurt from pushing the wheelchair, but not as bad as when I was lifting the bag.

"My car is right around the corner," she said heading for the back of the building. *Why is her car parked behind the store?* I wondered. *Is she just shielding her car from the fire or is there another reason?*

"Here," she said popping the trunk, and setting her two suitcases into it. "Now, I need you to step in there as well."

Two men jumped from behind the dumpster and grabbed my arms and started shoving me into the trunk, I tried to scream, but one of them shoved his hand over my face. I tried to kick back, but the pain in my rib cage increased and I collapsed into the trunk. I couldn't fight

Now I'm not sure if it was because of the pain in my rib cage or because it really happened that way but what I saw next sent my head spinning.

Open mouth hanging, drooling, mumbling Travis came out of that wheel chair like he had never been in one in his life. The suitcase and garment bag were thrown on one guy and he threw himself onto the other.

"Run, Amy!" he yelled as he threw his fists into the guys face.

I was just climbing out of the trunk when the lady that had led me to the car came around it with a gun pointed in my face.

"Stay in that trunk if you don't want your head blown off."

I froze. I looked in misery as one guy held Travis and the other one punched him in the face. Travis crumpled and was shoved in the trunk with me and the lid was slammed shut.

"Travis?" I whispered. Nothing.

We were captives in a car trunk and being driven to who knows where. My side hadn't quit throbbing yet and my head was spinning. What had just happened?

# CHAPTER 15
# THE HIDEOUT 🚓

*Oh, God, please help me.* I pleaded silently. I could feel
Travis since we were lying back to back, but he wasn't
moving. *Please help Travis.* I prayed.

"Travis?" I asked again, as I shook his shoulder.

"I'm not going anywhere," he muttered.

"Oh, you're awake," I said. "How do you feel?"

"I don't know why you were talking to me if you thought I
was asleep, but yes, I'm awake. And I'm feeling like two men
just pounded my face."

"Since we aren't going anywhere, would you mind
explaining a few things? I mean I thought you needed a
wheelchair and that you were…"

"That I was mentally slow?" he finished for me. "Maybe I
am, but not to the extent that you thought. You see all my life
I've heard bad things about my dad, and when I found out
that Mom was sending me out here, I wasn't very happy
about it. So when Dad sent two plane tickets, I asked Mom to
let Mike come with me. The whole reason I was coming was
to prove that Dad hadn't changed so that Mom could, in good
conscience, get a divorce."

"You were coming just to prove that your dad was a jerk?" I asked in disbelief.

"Yeah. And on the plane, Mike and I got this idea. We thought that if I acted like I was handicapped, than I could hear stuff about my dad that people wouldn't tell me if I was normal. I thought that people wouldn't be afraid to talk in front of me because they wouldn't think that I understood. I also thought that Dad couldn't love me if I was handicapped, so I figured that would give me another reason to tell Mom to go on with the divorce. Mike was a huge help."

"Where did you get the wheelchair?" I asked.

"We're actually renting that from the airport. I wasn't going to tell anyone here that I was normal, but you didn't leave me much choice."

"Well, thank you. I hope we live long enough for you to meet your dad again. He really is a great guy."

"I heard your description when you were telling me about him."

I felt the heat rising in my cheeks when Travis mentioned how I had told him about his dad. I'm sure I had looked crazy. Fortunately the darkness in the car trunk hid my red face.

"We need a plan," Travis said.

"What kind of a plan?" I asked.

"A plan to get out of here. Neither of us are tied up, but I don't think that will give us any advantage, they have guns, and even if they didn't, they're bigger and stronger than we are. We need another plan."

"Even if we did fight, they would probably kill us," I said.

"I know, so maybe we should pretend to be unconscious. Then they might not tie us up, and they might not watch us as close, and then we could escape."

"Sounds good. But promise me that if they keep me and leave you where you can get away, you will," I said slowly. I knew that it was probably my rib that they were after. Maybe The Surgeon himself was sitting in the car that we were in.

"Only if you promise me the same."

I paused. I didn't know if I could promise that.

"If you were tied up, and I was free, I would try to free you," I said.

"My feelings exactly," Travis said. "Now be quiet, we don't want them to hear us talking or they'll know that we aren't unconscious."

There was a long silent pause where the only sounds I could here were the spinning of the wheels and the murmuring coming from the front of the car. Then I felt a nudge.

"Psst. Amy."

"I'm still here," I said.

"Why don't you pray?"

I paused was he teasing me? Was he just trying to make sport of me being a Christian? Then I realized that no matter what he was doing it didn't matter, what mattered was that I trusted God.

"Dear God," I prayed in a whisper. "Travis and I could really use some help. I know you'll take care of us, but please, don't let them hurt us. Please help Dad find us, and please, give us peace. Amen."

There was another long pause. Then he spoke again.

"Thank you, Amy. Amy, I uh… I know Mike can be a bit irritating, and I don't agree with all of his teasing, but he's my friend."

"No need to apologize for your friend's behavior. That's his business." I paused. "What about you? How do you feel about spiritual stuff?"

He didn't answer me for a while. "I don't know," he finally said. "I've always felt just like Mike, but when I saw him tease you, and you responded with love instead, it made me wonder… I could tell you wanted to fight back, but you didn't. I respect anything that makes a person like you and your family. And I can tell that when you guys pray, stuff happens."

"If you're ever ready to take the next step, just let me know. We don't have any guarantees about tomorrow you know," I said solemnly.

"I know, I'm just not ready yet. You can pray for me though. If there is a God out there somewhere, I want his help if he can give it to me."

"He can, Travis, I think he already has. Talk to your dad about it. He would love to share with you how he's changed."

"When I see my dad, I need you to keep your mouth shut. I want him to think that I really am slow. If he can love me when I can give him nothing in return, than I might be able to trust him enough to let him talk to my mom."

"He's worthy of your love, Travis" I said.

"Shhh," he said. I felt the motion of the vehicle change, and suddenly I was thrown into Travis' back. The pain that tortured my rib cage was severe enough that I didn't think I was going to have to pretend to be unconscious. Why had the pain in my ribs been so much worse these last few weeks?

"I think we're stopping," he hissed, and I bit my lip to keep back an outburst of pain. How could I be thankful if this pain continued? And what if it got worse?

We had pulled off onto a bumpy road, and we pulled to a stop. When the trunk lid opened, I was grabbed by one of the two men and Travis was grabbed by the other. I know I was supposed to have my eyes closed, but I wanted to know where we were, so I squinted enough to be able to see that we were in a town, but not Rifton. We were next to an apartment building, that from the looks of it hadn't been used in at least twenty years. This whole section of town was very run down.

The woman took the car around the corner, and we were hauled into the house. I really did try to act limp, but with the tormenting pain ravaging through my side I'm afraid I kept tensing up. From what I could see, Travis was doing a great job pretending to be unconscious, but then that didn't surprise me, he was a great actor.

We were brought up to the third floor, and into an apartment room. I had given up playing limp since it was so obvious that I wasn't. Looking around the room, I surveyed my surroundings. Travis had been dumped in a heap on the floor, and I had been set in a chair near the back of the room. There were three doors going from the room. One was the exit, and since we were in the kitchen, I figured that the other rooms were probably a bedroom and a living room, or maybe a bathroom, I didn't know and I didn't care.

All that mattered was survival. I just had to take the next breath, to live, and to hang on until help came. One of the guys went over to the cupboard and started pulling out some food. He sat down and made himself a sandwich and started to eat right there. And the other one just stood by the door with his arms crossed.

The man eating at the table seemed a little over weight. His pudgy cheeks worked up and down as he chewed. He seemed like he was just there to do what he was told and to get money. But the guy by the door was a different story. He seemed to be the boss. He looked a little bit like the sheriff, and I wondered if he was the man that Paul had seen. But no, this man could not be Jim's dad. He looked too cruel.

Finally after what felt like two years the woman came in carrying the two suitcases that I had been helping her with.

"I hid the car. They won't know that we're here," she said to the man standing by the door who nodded in satisfaction.

"Now you know what you need to do. Do you have what you need?" he asked.

"I'm not paid to be stupid," the woman said coolly. She walked over to the table and shoved the food onto the floor.

"Hey, back off," the big guy at the table said.

"Shut up and do what she says," Lean face said.

"I need this table clean," she said glancing at me. I didn't like the look in her eye.

She pulled a coil of rope out of one of the suitcases, and cut off a big piece.

"Tie him up and stick him in the back room," she said gesturing toward Travis. "We don't need him."

Big guy went over and started to tie Travis up, while lean guy gagged him. Together they carried him into the back room.

I wanted to get up and try to make a run for it while they were in the other room, but every time I tried to move, I got such intense pain in my side that I couldn't move.

"Now, I want this clear before we start," the woman said putting her hands on her hips. "I'm going to get half of what we find is that right?"

Lean face smirked. "You get whatever I give you. I don't owe you anything."

"But you've been using my name for the last few months. You've given me a reputation that I don't like," she said.

"Look, I'm doing you a favor. Thanks to me, everyone now thinks that 'The Surgeon' is a guy. Me. No one has any clue that it's you. So, I would say you owe me something."

I inhaled sharply. This awful woman was The Surgeon.

"I just want you to know that without me you can't do this properly," she said staring him down. "I always scared people, but I never once killed people unnecessarily."

"What about that plane that you're sending down?" Lean guy said crossing his arms again.

"I'm sending it down, because it will cover the evidence that I poisoned Mayor Whitfield. He will die about the same time that the plane reaches the ocean, and it will be then that it goes down, in such a deep spot that it won't be recovered for a long time. And with him out of the way, we can do what we want with the town."

"You're forgetting, that was my idea," he retorted.

"True, but you owe me your life. I'm the one who got you out of jail. You miserable wretch you owe everything to me. So am I right in saying that I will get half of whatever we find?"

"Sure," he said. "But remember, I didn't have to do this your way at all. I would have just killed her and taken the rib out of her dead body. But since you insist upon keeping her alive, go for it."

I cringed. They would have to kill me to get my rib, but that was just what the woman had said they weren't going to do.

"Tie her to the table," the woman said. I hunched down in the chair as the two guys came toward me.

"No!" I screamed. I couldn't just let them tie me to a table in a dingy apartment in the middle of a deserted complex and remove my rib. No, I would fight despite the pain.

I kicked the fat guy in the knee, and then pulled myself to the floor and screamed at the top of my lungs. I kicked and screamed like a little kid. Or maybe like a desperate person.

The lean guy back handed me across the mouth and I stopped screaming, instead I licked the blood from the inside of my lip. But I wasn't going to quit kicking.

I put up the best fight that I knew how to, but somehow, they managed to get me laid across that table face down with one arm tied to each of the front legs, and each of my feet tied to the back legs of the table. I couldn't move.

The woman came around to the side that my face was looking, and waved a knife in my face.

"They don't call me The Surgeon for nothing. Don't worry, I know how to operate, but since we never got that envelope, we don't know which rib it is. Will you tell me?"

I shook my head as best as I could.

"Of course, I could just take them all out. That would save us the trouble of patching you back up," she said as she twisted the knife in a deadly fashion in the air. "So, which one is it? Will you tell me? Or should I just kill you and take them all out?"

I didn't have to think about that option. "It's the middle fixed rib on my right side," I said. "But how do you know about that?"

"I have my ways. Some little ears really do have big mouths. I couldn't help but hear Steve bragging about the treasure that he had gotten, I have my ways. Now which rib was it again?"

"The middle fixed rib on the right side," I said reluctantly.

"Thank you. You've been most helpful. Now, if I was you, I would grit my teeth, this will hurt," she said walking over to my right side. "It seems that I've forgotten my chloroform, but since you can't move, I don't think I'll have any trouble. And just remember, if you do move, I might accidently stab your heart."

Sweat dripped down my face. Where was Dad when I needed him? *God, please don't let this happen!* I begged. *God, I want to be thankful, but how? This isn't included in everything is it? Because I don't think I can give thanks for this.*

"You're not doing surgery on her while she's conscious are you?" the big guy asked.

"How else would you do it? I'm quite confident that I can do any surgery on any one at any time," she bragged. "Just be quiet."

"May I leave the room?" he asked. "I don't do well with blood."

"Then please, leave," the thin guy said as he came around the table. "It would be a shame to do something like this to a conscious person," he said and he lifted his fist.

The first punch hit me square on the cheek and since I couldn't move at all it threw my head back and there was a popping sound.

As the pain shot through my head, I finally thanked God. *Thank you for saving me. I prayed. Please don't let me die but thank you for loving me.* The second punch landed on my jaw, and I fell into the most unsweet sleep I had ever had. Unconsciousness.

# CHAPTER 16
# DEATH WOULD BE SWEET 🚓

I had thought that the pain in my side before could be matched by nothing. I was wrong. When I awoke, there was the worst torturous burning in my side. Apparently The Surgeon didn't have any pain killers either.

I had such an intense pain in my side that I didn't dare move. Breathing hurt, but that was a necessity. I could hear voices but they seemed distant and far away. As my head cleared, I began to realize that it was The Surgeon and the lean guy talking to each other.

I cautiously opened one eye, and was met by the grimmest sight that I had ever seen. Inches from my face, was a pile of rags covered in blood… my blood.

I slowly moved my eyes. Next to the pile of rags was my fake rib. It was broken in two, and standing next to it, was The Surgeon and the lean guy looking over a paper. I inhaled sharply, and then couldn't suppress the groan that came.

"Hey, she's awake," lean guy said.

"It's a miracle that she would wake up at all after you pounded her face like a boxing bag. She probably has brain swelling. Are you even alive?" she asked me as she stuck her face up next to mine.

"I must be. I hurt too much to be dead," I muttered while trying not to move or breath.

"Well, it's a good thing we kept you alive. We're going to need you," she said stepping back and scanning the paper she held.

I squeezed my eyes shut to keep the light from boring into my aching head.

"It seems that your old man left you a fortune. And with you and this paper, we can have it," The Surgeon said with a sneer in her voice. "Now, I patched you up perfectly well. There's no reason you need to sit there and act like you're dead," she said pulling the blood crusted knife from its case and slicing the ropes that bound me to the table. "Get up and eat something, we need you looking alive when we leave."

I wasn't sure if I had heard her right. She didn't really want me to get up did she?

"Morgan, help her."

The lean guy called Morgan walked over and started to pull me up to a sitting position. I couldn't contain the scream of pain as my whole body was wracked with a burning fire within. I tensed for a moment, and then slumped against Morgan. I didn't have the strength to do anything else.

"What is wrong with her? You can live without a rib. And I did a good job," The Surgeon said coming over to me. She held up a bright light, and shined it into my eyes.

I wanted to fight back, but every breath was a battle, and there was no way I could muster enough strength to do anything.

The Surgeon's skilled fingers ran over my side, and I could feel that her hands were cold all the way through my shirt. Her fingers hit a tender spot and I screamed.

The Surgeon pulled her fingers over the spot again and then stepped back.

"She's broken a rib. I suppose between a broken rib and a removed rib she's probably in a lot of pain."

Pain. That's all I felt. I was having trouble getting sensible thoughts. Had she just told me that I had a broken rib? How could I have broken rib? I remembered the excruciating pain that had run through my ribs when I had been tied to the table and I wondered if maybe I had somehow smashed it while laying on it.

"It won't help her to lie on her rib. Put her on that chair," The Surgeon ordered.

Morgan picked me up the rest of the way and I blacked out.

I opened my eyes. I was sitting in a soft reclining chair in the corner of the kitchen. Morgan and The Surgeon were still talking over the paper that they held.

From this angle, I could see the table that I had been lying on. It had blood splattered on it. That explained why I felt so light headed and disoriented.

"We need to go," Morgan said shoving some of The Surgeon's tools into one of the open suitcases on the floor.

"Careful!" she yelled at him. "Here, I'll get these. You go get that weak livered friend of yours." She started to gently place her instruments into the bag. Many of them had my blood on them.

Morgan came back with a large suitcase and set it on the table. He was being followed by the big guy, but when the big guy saw the table, he turned white. He leaned against the door post and looked at me. He clutched at his throat and made odd gasping noises.

The Surgeon shut her suitcase and handed it to the big guy. "Take this and get out of here. You'll only mess stuff up. Go get the car and pull it around back. We'll be down in a little bit."

I couldn't breathe without unbelievable pain shooting up and down my entire chest and rib cage. I found myself just wishing that they would leave me there to die. It would hurt a lot less than what I was feeling.

After collecting a few more items, Morgan grabbed the two suitcases from off the floor and started for the door.

"Stop you fool," The Surgeon said coming into the room with a blanket. "Take this down to the car and make a nice little nest in the trunk. We don't want our prize getting damaged in transportation, and then I need you to come back up here and help me. I can't carry her by myself, and she isn't walking."

Morgan's jaw tightened. "I'm the one giving the orders around here," he snapped.

"Don't be stupid, if it weren't for me, you would be in jail now," she said in a buttery voice. "You had better do as I say."

I saw a look of extreme hate cross Morgan's face, but he left and went to do as he was told.

Then I thought of Travis. I had said that if I was loose I would try to get him free. Well I was loose, but there was no way that I was ever going to be able to move on my own.

"Can we please take him with us?" I asked and nodded toward the room where they had left Travis tied up.

"Why? We don't need him. He'll only get in the way," she said with such an attitude of indifference that I knew she wasn't going to take him, but I had to try.

"Please, if you take him with us, I'll do whatever you want."

She laughed. "Trust me, you're going to do what I say if he's with you or not."

I didn't answer, she was right. I was in no position to bargain. I didn't have much of a choice but to do what she said. I was going to have to try to find a soft spot in her heart.

"Do you have a son?" I asked.

"No," was her short reply.

"Well, if you did, would you want him left tied up all alone just waiting for death?"

She paused for a minute, and I thought I had found her soft spot.

"No, I wouldn't. I would rather they shoot him," she said grinning. That definitely wasn't her soft spot. When Morgan came back, she pulled out a handgun.

"Morgan. The kid had a great idea. We need to shoot that boy in there, so that if anyone finds him he won't talk," she said calmly. My stomach churned. It would have been better if I hadn't opened my mouth at all. "Bring him in," she said.

Morgan gave her a look of disdain at being told what to do, but he went into the other room and came back dragging a fighting Travis. Travis' hands were tied behind his back, but he didn't let that stop him from making things difficult.

"Well, Kid. Your friend here thinks that it would be best if we shot you," she said with an evil grin on her lips.

Travis stopped struggling and stared at me with wide eyes. His look changed from a wide eyed look to a look of disbelief. I shook my head at him and pleaded with my eyes. Travis pulled away and thrust himself at Morgan. Morgan moved out of the way, and for a moment Travis wavered. Without his hands for balance, Travis couldn't break his fall as he fell onto the blood stained table.

"Let's go," The Surgeon said grabbing Travis' arm.

Morgan picked me up and I screamed as I tried to suppress the pain. We got out into the hall, and The Surgeon did the very thing that I was afraid of. She let go of Travis.

Travis ran down the hall. He started reeling before I even heard the gun shot. He fell on his back and I saw blood on the front of his shirt.

"Come on," she said walking toward the exit sign.

Hot tears streamed down my face, and I wasn't sure if they were from the pain or from what I had just seen. I think they were from both.

We were on the second landing going down when The Surgeon stopped to look out the window, and I was bumped into the wall sending another burst of pain through my upper body.

I'm not sure if it was the pain or the tears in my eyes, but I didn't see whatever it was that lit a fire under The Surgeon. She jumped back and screamed at Morgan.

"Why didn't you tell me that we were discovered?"

Morgan started to answer but he was cut off.

"It doesn't matter now, we need to act fast. Run back to our room and make sure we don't leave anything behind."

Morgan stuck his chin out. "The moment I go back, you're going to make a break for it without me." Morgan shook his head. "Sorry Pal, but I'm not being left behind."

The Surgeon was almost purring like a kitten. "I would never leave you behind. I'm just going to go check and see how bad it is," she said sweetly.

Morgan glared at her for a moment, and then took off running with me up the stairs. Every step sent new pain through my body, and I was battling for consciousness.

When we got to the landing on the third floor I noticed three things. One, right below the window there were four policemen climbing the fire escape. Two, Travis was nowhere to be seen, and three, there were two policemen standing at the other end of the hall heading towards us.

# CHAPTER 17
# UNPREPARED 🚓

Morgan dashed down the hall, but before we got into their range, he turned into the apartment that we had been using and locked the door behind him.

He dropped me on the floor and headed for the window. I'm not sure what he saw out the window since I was writhing in pain on the floor but I could tell that he wasn't going to be able to escape through it.

My rib still lay on the table, and my blood stained the table and floor. It made my stomach flip. I had been in excruciating pain since the moment that I had been captured, but the pain was escalating to a level that I couldn't bear.

I couldn't help but moan.

"Shut up," Morgan hissed. "We don't want them knowing which door we went in." He clamped a hand over my mouth, but I'm pretty sure he wished he hadn't. I heaved a couple of times and I felt myself blacking out from the pain, but I couldn't stop it, and I vomited into his hand.

His hand flew back, and I lost it. My stomach felt better, but the other pains were so intense that I passed out.

I couldn't have been out for more than a few minutes when I opened my eyes. All I saw was complete blackness. I didn't dare try to move and I didn't even care if I could.

I could tell that I was in some small place, A casket maybe. But the darkness seemed to be caused by a cloth over my eyes, was I blind folded?

I suddenly became aware of the fact that someone was in this coffin with me. I could feel something warm against my arm.

I cleared my throat and then waited for whoever it was to make themselves known.

"Are you awake?" the voice said, but I was much too groggy to know who it was.

"I think so," I muttered.

"This is going to hurt Amy, but you'll feel better if you drink something, so I'm going to prop you up okay?"

I didn't say anything, so whoever it was gently put one hand under my shoulder and the other under my mid-back and pulled.

I screamed. Whoever it was pushed a pillow behind me and let go. I fell back into an upright position against a pillow. The cloth fell from my eyes, and I saw the worried face of Travis.

Was the pain causing me to hallucinate? "You're supposed to be dead," I whispered between clenched teeth. "I saw your blood."

"That's just what it looked like," he said. "See this?" he said pulling on his shirt and pointing out the blood stain. "That's your blood. I got it on my shirt when I fell on the table, and when I knew that they were going to shoot me anyway, I decided to try to avoid getting shot and just act like I was hurt. I fell down, and at that moment The Surgeon pulled the trigger. I was really lucky that I fell at the right moment, or the bullet really would have hit me."

"That wasn't luck, Travis," I whispered through clenched teeth. "That was God looking out for you." *Thank you, God.* I finished silently.

"Call it what you will, but I never got hurt. I got up as soon as you left and came back here to get a knife to cut my ropes. When I was free, Morgan came back in here with you."

"Where are we?" I asked as I once again noticed that we were in a very tiny space.

"We're in the closet," he said holding a bottle of water up to my lips. "Morgan is in the other room trying to think of a way out. He didn't see me under the table, so as soon as he dumped you in here, I came in here after you. We're not locked in, but I think we're safest here."

I tried to sip the water without killing myself, but it was really hard. I tried to comprehend what had happened.

"Why was there a cloth on my face?" I asked.

"I put that there. It isn't fun to wake up and have light streaming in your eyes. I know it isn't very bright in here, but I didn't want to give you a headache as well."

"Don't worry. You couldn't give me a headache worse than the one that I already have," I moaned. I slowly lifted my left hand towards my head. Even that motion caused pain and I let my hand fall back in place.

I shut my eyes and tried to relax. I couldn't take a deep breath without pain, so just lying there not breathing was the best. Every breath caused unbearable pain, but since I had to breathe, I had pain.

Suddenly a shaking and pounding shook my body and I had to fight back the urge to scream.

"They must be breaking down the door to get in here," Travis said standing up in the small space. He cracked open the door. "Yep, that door is going to break any moment." He looked around a bit more, and then he stepped out of the closet and up to the door.

"Don't shoot!" he said in a firm voice. "I'm opening the door."

I could see through the open closest door that Travis was on his knees and reaching up to get the lock. He unlocked it and then scooted back to the closet doors.

The door was burst open and three grim faced officers burst in with guns drawn. Jim was at the lead, and even though his face was still full of fear he had a little bit more of a calm attitude about him than the last time I had seen him.

Travis motioned to the other room. And the officers started toward it, but then Jim stopped them. He motioned them back into the hall and sent Travis with them.

"Stay out," he said. "This is private. I want to take him alive." The other officers didn't question him, but I could tell they weren't just leaving. They stood in the door way with their guns still in their hands.

Jim flattened himself against the wall behind where the door would swing if Morgan opened it.

"Come out with your hands up, and we won't shoot," he said in a very commanding voice.

"Not on your life," Morgan yelled back. "If you want me, you have to come and get me."

The moment that Morgan started talking, Jim turned white. His gun hand was trembling and his jaw clenched until his veins stuck out.

Jim took a deep breath, and then spoke.

"Dad," he said quietly. "It's me, Jim."

Silence reigned in the apartment room. A gun sounded off somewhere else in the building but it seemed far away. All that mattered was what I had just heard. Morgan was Jim's real dad.

Finally I heard a much softer voice yell back.

"Jimmy?"

"That's right, Dad. I've been adopted, but I still carry the Trams name with pride. I'm a sheriff now, Dad, and it's my duty to arrest you. Please come out." Jim's voice was soft, almost pleading. His face was contorted into all kinds of different emotions, and there were tears in his eyes.

There was another long pause.

"I'm not coming out, Jimmy. You come get me, and I'll shoot you," Morgan yelled back in his normal rough voice.

Jim's gun hand fell limply at his side and he stepped out into the hall. I could hear his every word.

"Men, he's in that room. Chances are that the first few men into that room will go down with him. I'm willing to be the first, but if any of you have any other plans I'm happy to hear them."

There was a short pause when Travis spoke up. He was whispering and I couldn't hear him.

The sheriff was silent for a bit and then he agreed. Two of the men left, and Jim, Travis, and another officer came back into the room.

The other officer, whom I recognized as Officer Will, stood with his gun aimed at the closed bedroom door, but Jim looked around the room.

"What happened here?" he asked as he chipped up a bit of dry blood with his thumbnail.

Travis picked up the dreaded fake rib and handed it to Jim. "What is this?" he asked.

"They removed that from Amy's rib cage," Travis said calmly.

Jim dropped the rib on the table with a clatter and stared at it.

"Is she…" he didn't finish his sentence because at that moment his eyes fell on me. He ran over to the closet and pulled the doors open so that I now had a full view of the other room.

Jim dropped to his knees by me "Amy… Amy I…Are you…" his voice was shaking.

"I'll be fine," I said through my clenched teeth, but it didn't take a rocket scientist to tell that I was in great pain.

"Is there anything I can do?" The look on Jim's face was pure sympathy and grief. He blamed himself for what his dad had done.

"I'll be okay," I said trying to smile.

Jim didn't look at all convinced. "It isn't safe for you to be here," he said glancing at the adjoining door going to the bedroom. "I don't want you here when he comes out. He might kill you. We need to get you out of here. Do you think you can walk?"

I couldn't help but snort. I inhaled sharply at the pain it had caused, and when the pain finally subsided slightly, I whispered. "I'm sorry, Jim, but I can hardly breathe. If I'm going to be moved, you are going to have to carry me, and I'm probably going to scream the entire time."

Jim rubbed his chin trying to think of a way to move me.

"Just because I'm in pain doesn't mean that you can't move me. Go ahead," I said.

I never did figure out why I told Jim he could move me. I think it was the dumbest thing I have ever done.

I didn't have to worry about screaming the whole time because after the pain of being picked up, I passed out and was completely silent.

When I woke up, Travis was sitting by my side and I was lying on the floor in what probably used to be a living room, I mean it was carpeted.

"What's going on?" I asked.

"You know as much as I do." He said. "Sheriff Trams told me to stay here with you until he comes back for us. Which if I'm right, may be a while."

"What are they going to do?" I asked.

"They're going to take a rope and lower someone down from the window on the fourth floor that is right above the window of the room that Morgan is in, and whoever they lower down is going to stick a tear gas bomb into the window. Either Morgan will come out on his own accord, or he will be put into a state where he can be easily apprehended."

My head was spinning. My throat was burning, and I had a really bad gut feeling, something wasn't right, I could feel it.

"Are you sure we're safe here?" I asked.

Travis shrugged, "as safe as we are going to be anywhere else," he said.

I couldn't shake the feeling that something was wrong. Something was really wrong.

I prayed fervently in my heart that God would let us live through this, but I still couldn't shake the feeling.

"What's wrong, Amy?" Travis asked when he noticed that I was sweating. "There's nothing to worry about. Morgan can't get to you unless he goes through Sheriff Trams. You're perfectly safe."

I tried to believe him, but I didn't feel right, something was wrong. Then I knew what it was.

"Where is The Surgeon?" I asked.

Travis shrugged. "I don't know, but I would assume that one of the other groups caught her."

"But what if they didn't?" I asked. "She could still try to use us as a hostage. Believe me, I've had enough of being someone's hostage for the rest of my life."

"Then I won't use you," the unmistakable voice of The Surgeon said. I cringed. Travis jumped to his feet, but when she stepped into the room, she had a gun pointed straight at me. Travis didn't want to upset her. "You say you don't want to be a hostage kid. Fine. I'll use you boy," she said reaching out and grabbing Travis' arm. She looked at me one last time. "If I get Morgan, we will be back for you. We need you," she said and then she was off down the hall with Travis.

I knew I needed to hide. I needed to get up and go somewhere else, somewhere safe.

Gritting my teeth I put every ounce of energy I could muster into getting up. I moved off the ground about two inches when my strength gave out and I fell back smashing my back into the carpet.

I was actually trembling. I felt like I was having a seizure or something.

The Surgeon would come up behind Jim and Officer Will, and make them let Morgan out. Then they would come and get me. They needed me for whatever heartless plan they had.

"God, help me," I begged. "I don't have any strength." I lay there thinking about what the Bible commanded me to do, *In EVERYTHING give thanks.*

I bit my lip, could I really thank God for this? *Oh God, I don't have the strength I need. Please give me strength.* I laid there for a few more moments and then grit my teeth. "Thank You for this pain. Thank You for this danger, and thank You for caring about me. Please give me strength." I laid there for a few more moments, and then gritting my teeth harder, I rolled over. I had to wait a few more moments before I could move again, but in a few minutes, I was on my knees. One more painful moment, and I was on my feet. I was leaning all my weight against the wall. I worked my way toward the hall, and then down it. I was sure I must look like a drunkard the way I was staggering.

I was just about to the door of the apartment when I fell to my knees. I didn't think I could make it another step, and yet I couldn't fall off of my feet now that I was on my knees. It was ironic. When I had been on my feet, I had been struggling all over the place, but now that I was on my knees, I was stable.

*Thank you, God.* I prayed silently.

I crawled around the corner and stopped short. The Surgeon was about two feet away from me with Travis in front of her.

"I'm not joking, Morgan, come out," she yelled.

Jim and Officer Will were both standing with their guns at their feet and their hands in the air.

It's funny the things you think of in situations like that. But at that moment, I couldn't help but think of how embarrassing it must be to be an officer and have your hands in the air like that.

"How do I know this isn't a trap?" Morgan called back.

"Just trust me okay?" The Surgeon yelled back.

There was a small pause, and I heard a window break.

"What in the…" Morgan yelled. A string of curses came from behind the closed door. The door between the two rooms burst open and Morgan came out with one hand over his eyes and his gun hand waving his gun in every direction.

I figured if I was going to do anything, I had to do it now, when he was confused, so I took a deep breath and lunged forward. When I hit the back of the Surgeon's knees, she collapsed.

You would think with the whole floor before her she could have found a better spot, but no. She had to land right on my back. As the pain overtook my body, I groaned in pain. *In Everything give thanks,* I remembered.

Her gun rose as soon as she caught her balance, but Travis had already lunged for that, and he now held the gun on her.

Morgan was still trying to see, but he knew enough to know that he was in trouble.

He shot toward the men, but praise God he couldn't see where he was aiming. Jim and Officer Will lunged in two different directions, and they both grabbed their guns.

Then Morgan saw me.

"It's all that girl's fault," he yelled, and he swung his gun to point at me. I could see that his finger was on the trigger and I heard a shot.

# CHAPTER 18
## PAIN 🚓

I couldn't tell if I had been hit or not. I don't think I would have felt any different if I had. I already was in the state of extreme misery. I don't know how things could have gotten worse.

I figured the gun shot must not have been Morgan's, since he was the one that fell.

I looked over to where Jim stood, gun in hand and tears streaming down his face.

Officer Will slammed the door shut to keep the gas from getting into our eyes, and then he grabbed The Surgeon and pulled her off of me and handcuffed her.

Travis knelt by me. "Are you alright?" he asked.

I didn't even try to answer. I didn't even lift my chin from the floor. I just blinked. I hoped that he would take that as a nod.

I looked at Jim, and saw him kneeling on the floor with Morgan's head in his hands.

"Dad," he whispered. His head was shaking and tears were streaming down his face. They weren't all from the tear gas either.

"Suspects three and four apprehended on the third floor," Officer Will said into his shoulder radio.

Within a few minutes, several more officers entered the room. They all had to step over me to get into the room, and I was sure they thought I was dead.

Officer Tony tried to give me medical attention, but The Surgeon had wrapped me up very well. There was nothing he could do.

When he was done, he went over to check on Morgan, but it was too late. Officer Tony put his hand on Jim's shoulder, and gently squeezed it.

"We stopped the plane, and got the mayor to a hospital. He's going to be alright," Officer Tony said cheerfully in an attempt to cheer Jim up, but Jim wouldn't even open his eyes.

I didn't know if it would work, but I only knew one thing that might be an encouragement to Jim. I wasn't about to try to say a sentence, but maybe I could manage one word.

"Grace," I said. I'm afraid it came out more like "Grr." Several of the officers gave me strange looks, but Jim got the message. He took a deep breath, and sighed. Then he stood to his feet wiped a hand across his eyes and walked toward me.

Kneeling beside me, he stared into my eyes. There was pain written all the way into the depths of his eyes, but it was a different kind of pain than I was experiencing. Finally he looked up.

"Men, I know you don't all agree with me, but it is my habit to thank God for everything. So if you will excuse me, I'm going to pray. That doesn't mean you have to take your eyes off of the prisoner. God can hear you just as well when your eyes are open."

Jim was met by murmurs of affirmation and some of disgust, but everyone in the room got quiet. Those that agreed with Jim got to their knees as well, and Jim thanked God. He thanked God that we were all still alive, and he thanked God for giving him the strength he needed.

When he was done, five officers took The Surgeon down to the cars, and medics showed up and put me onto a stretcher. It hurt, but they gave me something for the pain, so it turned to just an intense numbing pain.

Jim never left my side, neither did Travis.

"I thought you asked your God to protect us?" Travis asked as I was being carried down to the ambulance. "Why didn't He?"

"He did," I mumbled. "If God hadn't been in charge, I would be dead right now." My speech sounded slurred even to me.

Travis was quiet for a few more steps.

"You really trust God, don't you?" he finally asked.

"With all my heart, Travis. He loves me more than anyone else ever could. I know He wants what's best for me," I said.

Travis just grunted, and I prayed for him silently. It was my dream for every one of my cousins to know Christ personally.

I was just about to the ambulance when a police truck showed up and six guys piled out.

"Dad!" I whispered when I saw him.

He came running to my side, and squeezed my hand. "I'm not your dad, Amy. Your dad went to check on your mom. I'm your Uncle Luke."

Twins, you never can tell who you're talking to.

The change on Travis' face when Uncle Luke said that was very noticeable. He stiffened up, and his eyes narrowed to little slits.

He slowly walked around until he stood a mere three feet from his dad.

"Son," Uncle Luke said gently. "I'm sorrier than you will ever know about the past, and I want to make it up to you. Are you alright?" he asked while stepping toward Travis with his arms open.

Travis took a step back. "I'm as good as every other kid whose dad leaves him," Travis said bitterly.

Everyone was quiet, it was a rather awkward situation and I think everyone wished that they could have had this conversation in private.

Travis stared at his dad's open arms for a few seconds, and then he stepped forward, but instead of hugging his dad, his fist flung out and he punched Uncle Luke right on the jaw.

Uncle Luke gently rubbed his chin with one hand and looked directly into Travis' defiant gaze.

"I still love you, Travis. There is nothing you can do to make me wish I wasn't your father. Son, I love you."

Travis' eyes wavered. It was obvious that he had thought his dad would get mad at him.

Travis stared for another second, and the silence hung in the air. Then he jumped forward again and punched his dad in the stomach, and then the nose. Officer Will stepped forward, but Jim held him back.

"It's a private fight," he said.

Uncle Luke wiped the blood from his nose, and smiled.

"I still love you."

"Why can't you just get mad?" Travis screamed and launched at him again. This time Uncle Luke bent down, so that his face was easier to reach, and Travis gave him another hard crack on the jaw.

"I can't get mad, because I'm not mad, Son, I love you. God has changed me."

Tears started to pool in Travis' eyes, and he blinked hard to keep them back.

"You love me?" he asked. His hands were still tightly clasped in fists. He held up a fist. "Look me in the face and say that you still love me," Travis' voice was hard, but his eyes were pooling with tears.

Uncle Luke looked Travis full in the eye and said with a smile on his face, "I love you, Son."

Travis melted. The dam broke and tears flowed down his face. Travis held back a moment longer, and then he flung himself into Uncle Luke's arms.

Uncle Luke hugged him back with tears streaming down his own cheeks.

I was placed in the back of the ambulance. My whole rib cage ached like someone had been beating on it with a baseball bat and I squeezed my eyes shut as I got another wave of pain from being rolled into the ambulance.

"Amy." I opened my eyes. It was Timothy. "We'll come visit you as soon as we can," he said, and I saw a tear run down his face. What was so wrong that made everyone cry when they saw me? Did I really look that bad?

"Thank you, Tim," I said in as firm a voice as I could muster, but I noticed that it still sounded weak and sickly. I tried to smile, but my cheeks felt stiff from the dried blood. All I could feel was pain.

# CHAPTER 19
# HOSPITALS AGAIN 🚑

I got my hearing back before anything else, and I heard a gentle murmur of voices coming from somewhere nearby. I felt numb all over, and when I tried to move my arm, nothing happened. I lay there for quite a while just hearing voices and feeling but not seeing or comprehending.

When I finally opened my eyes I realized that I had tubes all over me, and some of them had needles going into my arm.

I could feel tubes over my nose, and I could tell that I had some kind of a breathing tube attached to my nose. I blinked a couple of times, and then tried to turn my head.

There sitting on a small padded bench were my mom and dad. I can't even explain what that meant to me to be able to see them and know that they were my parents, and that they loved me enough to be there. At that moment all the sounds I had heard and what I saw somehow merged and I comprehended that I was awake.

But something wasn't right, Mom had been crying, and her eyes were still red, I could see tears still lingering in Dad's eyes as well.

I wasn't sure if I could talk, but I was going to try.

"Mom," I said. It came out as a mumble but she heard me. In a moment she and Dad were at my side.

They called in a doctor, and he asked me several questions, I had a hard time talking, but I tried to answer as best I could. Yes, I knew who the president was, and no, I didn't know what day it was. A nurse took my blood pressure and I saw that I was hooked up to a machine that showed my every heartbeat.

"How do you feel?" Mom asked gently when the nurse left.

"Very numb," I said. My voice didn't sound right, it sounded far away and slurred, like I was talking through a paper towel tube. "I can't really move. What's wrong with me?" I asked as I began to wonder why I had all of these tubes hooked up.

Mom sniffed a little bit, and then she spoke.

"You've given us quite the scare. You're on your second blood transfusion."

"Well, that explains why I have the IV, but why do I have this tube thing in my nose?" I asked. As I spoke, my tongue felt thick and numb, like it does when the dentist accidently pokes it with Novocain.

"You stopped breathing, Amy."

I didn't really understand why they seemed so worried. What did they mean I had quit breathing? I felt almost fine. Well, at least way better than I had felt for the last few weeks, but then they wouldn't have any way of knowing that. They didn't know how often my ribs hurt.

"What was in my rib?" I asked as snippets of memory came back to me.

"It was the number of a bank box and the combination."

"What was in the box?" I asked.

"We don't know. The box had two different security systems, the one was the combination, and the other security setting requires your finger print. That's why they needed you alive. But don't worry. The Surgeon, as they call her is in jail for a long time, and so is that other guy."

"I should be ready to go in a day or two, and then we can see what's in that bank box," I said trying to smile.

Mom and Dad didn't smile.

"And then I want to see Travis and Uncle Luke too. How are they getting along?"

"Travis is home now, but after that first meeting, they got along famously together. I'm pretty sure that if Travis has any say in the matter they will be back together in no time. But he did come and see you several times."

"He's already home?" something didn't make sense. "How long have I been here?"

"It was seven days yesterday," Mom said gently.

If it hadn't been for all of those tubes and for the slightly numbing pain, I would have bolted upright.

"A week!" I said slowly trying to take it in. "What happened?" I asked. Even in my slightly confused zonked out state, I still knew that a simple removal of a rib shouldn't have put me unconscious for a week.

Dad pulled his chair up beside my bed and held my hand in his. He didn't start right away, he just stared at me. Then he looked away.

"What's wrong?" I repeated.

"I don't know how to tell you this, Amy. But you have bone cancer again. And it's bad."

As his words sunk in I felt like I was going back in time. I remembered another doctor passing the same diagnosis on me. I remembered the long months of treatment and surgery. I remembered the pain, and suddenly all of my rib pain over the last few months made sense.

"How bad?" I asked. "And when do they start treatment?"

"They've already done two surgeries. You had a reaction to some of the medication, and you went into a coma."

"When do they start the normal treatment?" I asked.

Mom walked around the bed and held my other hand. "We don't know, Amy," She said blinking back tears. "They might not."

"Why not?" I asked.

"It is a very advanced stage," Dad explained. "It seems like your entire rib cage is infected by it and some of your vertebrae as well. That's why your rib broke so easily, because it was full of cancer."

As Dad's words sunk in, I suddenly felt a fear wash over me. I had never been afraid of death before because every time that I had ever seriously faced it, it had been in a situation where it was me against someone else. Then all I had to do was hold out until the police got there. And the last time I had cancer it had been just hold out till the treatment was done.

But this was different. If my cancer really was to the stage that it was beyond treatment, then I would die slowly, and I couldn't fight it. Even when I had fallen out of the barn with

Steve, it had been my choice, and when I had been with The Surgeon, I knew that she wasn't going to kill me on purpose.

Even when Uncle Keith had pointed his gun at me, I had known that I wasn't dying until he pulled the trigger, and if he did pull it, then I would die in an instance. But this... it could take months.

"What stage am I at?" I asked.

"We're not sure yet. We have a meeting with the doctor in an hour, and he will give us the test results. He thinks it is in a late stage three. This means it hasn't started to affect your organs yet, but it could at any time."

I squeezed my eyes shut. I remembered what I had been told about hardship. 'You can get bitter or better' had been Jim's words. I sighed. I wanted to get better; even if it wasn't a physical better.

"Are you doing okay?" Dad asked as he squeezed my hand again.

"Yeah," I said, but even as I said it, hot tears ran down my face. I was the track champion in my old school, I was a runner, and I was active. I loved my movement, and my energy. How could God take that all away from me?

"May I come to the meeting?" I asked.

"Not unless the doctor comes here, but I think we're going to his office," Mom said wiping the tears from her eyes.

"But don't worry. Grace is going to come and sit with you while we're at the meeting. You won't be alone."

I liked the idea of getting to spend some time with Grace, but she isn't my mother, and I can't say having a sister at your side is anywhere near as comforting as a mother.

Dad read to me from Psalm chapter 119, and then we prayed together. Praying with Dad and Mom gave me a connection with them. And since we hadn't ever had any real connection time, it was really special.

"Amy. We're so sorry that we haven't really gotten to spend any time with you, but with everything going on, it just hasn't happened," Mom said sadly.

"Maybe now we can get to know each other better," I said trying to lighten up the moment, but it didn't work.

I talked and cried with Dad and Mom a lot in that hour. When they finally left, I prayed and asked God to let it only be a stage three, and I asked God to let them treat me so that I could get better. I knew that God would answer my prayer.

With Dad and Mom praying with me, I knew that God would hear us. I thanked God for giving me the parents that he had, and for getting me back with them before I knew about the cancer. Then I shut my eyes. I was so tired my eyes just wouldn't stay open.

When I finally opened my eyes, Grace was sitting at my side reading out loud, or was she? As I looked around the room, I saw Jim sitting on the other side of my bed, and he was laughing at something Grace had just said.

I could see a sparkle in both of their eyes, and I knew that everything was alright.

"When's the wedding?" I asked.

"Welcome back to the land of the living," Grace said smiling at me, but even through her smile, I saw sadness when she looked at me.

"You might want to do the wedding soon if you want me there," I said smiling.

Neither of them smiled. Grace wiped a tear from her face.

"We've known each other for ever it seems, there is no reason we should wait too long," Jim said smiling, and even though he still looked like he had too much responsibility, he looked ten years younger than the last time I had seen him.

"So, tell me what happened." I said, "How did they catch the big guy?"

"You must mean Carl Hansby. He was standing outside next to their getaway car, and he gave up without a fight."

"Didn't we hear a shot when we were there?" I asked.

"Yes, we did. But only one. That was our signal that one guy was out of the picture for the time being. But I tell you that apartment complex is huge, it was impossible to watch the whole thing at once."

"Why was it abandoned?" I asked.

"Good question, but the actual truth is that it was never used. The week they were going to start letting people in, they found out that they had an issue with their water system. For the last twenty years they've been going through red tape. The guy who built it died, and his son didn't want to run an apartment. And I guess you could say that since it's in such a dumpy part of town it got a lot of wanderers and drifters stopping in. When the owner saw what a state it was in he gave up on it and put it up for sale, but he was asking way too much for it. So there it sits just waiting for some rich person to buy it."

"What about the hotel? Is it alright? Was anyone hurt?" I asked when I remembered the whole reason I had been captured.

"It turned out to not be as serious as it looked. It did a bunch of damage, but nothing that can't be fixed. No one was seriously hurt."

"Can't we talk about something more cheerful?" Grace interrupted.

"When are your siblings coming?" I asked Jim. He ran his fingers through his hair.

"Jennie is coming in two weeks, and the other three are coming in one. Grace has been helping me fix up my house so that it's livable for kids. Not that they're kids, but you know."

I knew exactly what he meant. Jennie was fourteen, just like me, and the other kid that he had to take custody of was sixteen.

"So, these other kids seem very close knit." I remarked trying to make conversation.

"You can say that again." Jim said sighing. "The oldest one is twenty one years old, and the middle one is nineteen. Most twenty one and nineteen year olds aren't willing to move half way across the country just because their little sibling has a guardian up there, but they refuse to separate. But then I guess when you come from our situation, you have to cling to family. They can be all you have." Jim stared off into the distance.

"Jennie is really looking forward to seeing you again, Amy," Grace said.

It was hard to picture my best, and used to be only, friend Jennie as being Jim's little sister. She wasn't a thing like him. But then she grew up in a steady foster home.

We were laughing about Jim wearing a bow tie at his wedding, when Mom and Dad walked in. I choked on my laugh when I saw their faces.

Jim stood up and gave Mom his chair, and Dad stood at the foot of my bed with the most serious face I had ever seen.

"Well?" I asked.

I could tell by Mom's red eyes that it wasn't good.

"Do you want the long version or the short one?" he asked me.

"Give me the short one first, and then the long one," I said trying to swallow the lump in my throat.

Dad was chewing on his lip and looking out the window. I could see tell-tale lines of tears on his cheeks. Finally he spoke. "The Doctor said that he could not, in good conscience, tell us that you would live beyond next month. There's nothing they can do at this stage."

Grace's lip was trembling and her cheeks shone with tears. Mom was squeezing my hand like her life depended on it, and Dad was looking away but I could see his shoulders shaking. I looked at Jim and he also had tears sparkling on his cheeks.

Less than two months to live.

# CHAPTER 20
# DECISIONS 🚓

Dad went into a long explanation about how it was genetic and how his dad and grandma had both died of it, but I didn't really hear much of what he was saying. Mom and Grace were crying, but I was too stunned to cry.

As it began to sink in, my lips began to tremble. I had less than two months to spend with the family that I had only recently learned to love. Somewhere in the back of my head a verse kept repeating itself. *In EVERYTHING give thanks.*

"So there is no treatment," I repeated.

"The Doctor said that they could remove all of your rib bones and replace them, but he doesn't think it's possible to remove your vertebrae, so it wouldn't really help that much. They could do chemo, and he thought that if they did that then you might last another month, but he said you would probably be sick a lot of that time."

"We're not doing chemo," I said firmly. I had too many bad memories of that. The doctor was right, I would be sick the whole time.

"If we're not doing treatment, then can't they take these tubes off of me and let me go home?" I asked, but as I said it

I realized that I couldn't feel my legs at all, there was no way I was walking out of there. "What's wrong with my legs?" I asked.

"During one of the surgeries, when they were removing some of the cancer before they knew how bad it was, there was a complication. It seems that your spinal cord was somehow injured, and you're paralyzed from your waist down," Dad said in an unsteady voice. "They think that two of your vertebrae somehow pinched it."

I was stunned, even if I did live, I would never be able to walk again.

As the tears flowed down my cheeks I shook my head. This couldn't really be happening.

"I just want to go home," I cried.

Dad walked over to Mom's side and put his hand on her shoulder. Jim was standing behind Grace, and every one of them had tears flowing down their cheeks. It's strange, I know, but when everyone else is sad, it makes me want to cheer them up, so I smiled through my tears.

"Aren't you jealous?" I said, "I'm going to get to meet Jesus face to face before any of you."

That didn't help anyone stop crying, so I just decided to let myself cry with them.

They were all too afraid to hug me for fear that they would hurt me by bumping my tubes and IVs, but they hugged each other, and I wanted more than ever to just go home.

\*       \*       \*

"Please?" I begged.

"The answer is no," The nurse said firmly as she straightened my blanket at the foot of the bed.

"But if I'm dying anyway, is moving me and possibly ruining my spinal cord for good really going to matter? I would rather be sitting at home completely unable to move than here with a possibility of getting feeling back in my legs. Besides, I don't want to be able to feel. It would hurt too much."

The nurse stopped and looked at me. "I'm sorry, Amy, but you can't be moved. You need the equipment here, and we can't move all of our equipment to your home."

I hate to say that I was sulking, but after three days of sitting in a hospital room, (Well three days that I was conscious.) I was so sick of nurses and hospitals that I couldn't imagine staying there for the next month until my death. I was having a hard time being thankful for it.

My family had practically lived in my room, one of them was always with me, but right now they had all gone to church, so I was alone. I had a CD playing the Bible to me all morning. Actually, I had one playing almost constantly since I had been admitted to the hospital.

I was scheduled to Skype Travis that afternoon, but until then, it was just me and God, and of course the nurses that kept interrupting. Not that I'm complaining, they were doing a great job and I wouldn't have wanted to be there without them, but still, I don't like my room feeling like grand central station.

When the nurse left the room, I stared in frustration at the wall opposite my bed. I wanted to be running around outside not stuck in a hospital bed. I knew that I would probably never leave this hospital alive.

The worst part of it all was that my family wouldn't stop fussing over me. I love them more than I can express. But it is really hard having people crying over you all the time. And I knew that I was being a financial drain on them.

I knew that they didn't have a lot of money, and that they didn't have insurance, and that I was going to be a continual drain on them until the day that I died, and even then they would have to pay for my funeral. Funerals are expensive.

I didn't want my family to see me when I was dying, I knew the pain of cancer, and I didn't want them to have to see it. It isn't a pretty sight. I didn't want them having to see me get weaker. I didn't want them to have to spend every penny they owned on someone that was dying.

I had asked Jim to research for me to see if there was any place that I could go that would be cheaper. Somewhere where I could just call my family, and then one day the phone calls would stop coming, and they wouldn't have to go through dealing with my body and things. But Jim hadn't gotten back to me yet. I was pretty sure that even if he did find a place, Mom and Dad wouldn't let me go. They loved me too much for that, but it was out of my love for them that I wanted to go.

I spent a very boring morning like always, and when Paul came in with his laptop to hook me up to talk to Travis, I was ready for some company.

"How was church?" I asked.

"Good," he said.

"What went wrong?" I asked, knowing that if I wanted information I was going to have to use more pointed questions.

Paul looked up from his lap top. "Grace messed up on the third verse of 'The Love of God.' And Joe Pacs fell off the swing set and got a bloody nose."

I laughed. "I hope you didn't tell Grace that she messed up," I said smiling.

Paul shook his head. "I didn't have to tell her, everyone got on the wrong note and it was obvious."

"Well what went good?" I asked.

"We sang 'There is a fountain,'" he said.

"Do you like that song or something?" I asked.

"Yes, but that's not why it's good. It's good because Grace played the entire thing without looking at the music or the piano."

"What was she looking at?" Then I stopped, did I really need to ask? "Was it Jim?" I asked.

Paul nodded. "On a scale of one to ten, with ten being the highest, I would rate their love at about one hundred and ten."

I giggled. It was so good to know that everything was alright between them. Jim stopped by to see me every day, and he sent roses to Grace twice a week. Jim had started to look happier than I had ever seen him, and I was glad. It had been really hard for him having to shoot his dad. In fact, the whole ordeal with his family and the mayor, and the parole officer had really gotten to him. It was good to see him happy again.

"You're on," Paul said setting the lap top on my lap and pushing call. In moments Travis' face filled the screen.

"Hey!" he said. "I just had to talk to you and let you know how sorry I am that I didn't fight back. I should have never let them tie you up."

"It's okay. If you had fought back you wouldn't be alive today. Besides, I can honestly thank God for letting me go through that. If God hadn't let me go through that, I wouldn't know that I have cancer."

Travis was quiet for a bit. "Yeah, about that, how are you doing?" he finally asked.

I took a deep breath and let it out slowly. "You know what? I'm actually doing really well with it all. I mean I'm sick of being in bed already, but I have so much to be thankful for."

"Like what?"

"Like the fact that God let me come to my family before all of this happened, and that I have a home in Heaven and that I don't have to go through chemo. There are so many other things to be thankful for. I'm thankful for the time that I did have here on this earth. I can even thank God for my encounter with The Surgeon. There's a verse in I Thessalonians that says, 'In everything give thanks: for this is the will of God in Christ Jesus concerning you' and that's what I'm trying to do. Praise God for everything, and give thanks. Even when it's tough, and especially when it's tough."

"Are you scared?" he asked.

I paused. "Not about the being dead part. I know where I'm going. I just pray that God takes me while I'm sleeping. I think it would be the best thing in the world to wake up and be in Jesus' arms." I bit my lip how was I to word this? "Travis… Where are you going when you die?"

"Until yesterday I was going to Hell. But I was talking with Dad on the phone, and he shared his testimony with me again, and how he was forgiven. I knew that I was a sinner, and I wanted to have that relationship with God that he had, so I confessed my sins to God, and I gave myself all to Him."

"Praise God!" I almost shouted. "I've been praying for you."

"Thank you, I needed it, it was a tough decision. If you think of it, keep praying for Mike, as you know, he isn't a Christian, and pray for my parents."

"What's going on with them?" I asked.

"I came home with a glowing report about Dad, and Mom said she's willing to work on building a relationship with him. But right now her fuse is less than a centimeter, so Dad really has to tread lightly. And she isn't a Christian."

We spent the next half hour talking about everything under the sun, until he had to go. When he said good-bye, I was back to my wall staring routine.

Paul left with his computer and he said that Mom and Dad would be by to see me soon.

I shut my eyes and tried to think of all the blessings that I had. I had done that a lot lately. Life was hard enough without me complaining, but when I thanked God for everything, it made everything seem like not such a big deal. God was in control, and He had given me so much to be thankful for.

The door opened, but I didn't bother to open my eyes. I knew it was Mom.

"Hi Mom," I said waiting for her to kiss me and then ask why my eyes were shut.

Someone cleared their throat, and it wasn't Mom's throat, it was a deep male throat. I opened my eyes. Jim stood at the foot of my bed with a twinkle in his eyes and a smirk on his face.

"Mom?" he asked.

"Hey, Jim," I said smiling. "You're not going to tell everyone else are you?"

His eyes twinkled. "Not everyone else. But I might tell Grace."

"I would throw something at you if I had anything to throw, but since I don't, why don't you grab a seat and tell me about church. Maybe you could tell me more than Paul told me."

Jim sat down and looked off with that starry look in his eyes. "Well," he began. "Grace was wearing her tiered black skirt and a red sweater. Her hair was down, and it looked absolutely beautiful. She did an excellent job on the piano. I don't think she messed up at all."

I couldn't help but smirk. "Forget the descriptions, what brought you here today?" I asked.

"Can't I visit my little sister without being interrogated? What makes you think I'm not here just to visit you?" he said smiling that smile that made him look like a teenager. I had seen that smile a lot lately. I think it has something to do with Grace.

"You have your laptop with you, and you don't normally carry that without a reason."

"You ought to be a detective, Amy, but you're right, I'm here to show you something." He pulled his chair up to where I could see what he was doing on his computer screen, and he leaned over and pointed things out to me.

"This is the Ned home. It's a small annex to a large Christian medical college in Missouri. It was named after a man named Ned who had a vision to see medical research done. It is mostly a place where they take corpses for medical research."

"I'm not dead yet," I cut in.

"I know that, Amy, but a few years ago they built a small wing for live patients. It's a place where college students can do research and experiments on the patients. It's mostly people who are dying and don't have any family. It's a Christian home, and they are mostly well advanced students who are trying to find cures for diseases.

They don't allow more than ten patients at a time, and they have a few openings. The good news is, this place is practically free. These students want so badly to be able to help the world by finding cures to things like brain swelling, or late term cancer. They will work for hours in this place with little or no pay, all in the name of education."

I sat back, and would have crossed my arms if I could have, but the IV's prevented that, and even if they hadn't, I couldn't lift my hands without pain.

"So, you want me to just let these college kids do experiments on me?" I shook my head in disbelief. I had given Jim more credit than that.

"You don't understand. It's not like they don't know what they're doing. The reason I'm so excited about this, Amy, is because my sister, Jodi, had a lung disease that is said to be fatal. She actually just got out of that home, and although she isn't cured, she is still alive and the doctors say that she should live for several more years. Before she went to that home, they said that she wouldn't live for more than a few weeks. My point is, they may be able to help you." I could feel the excitement in Jim's voice, but I wasn't ready to accept it quite yet.

"You say that it's practically free?" I repeated.

"Yep, and they provide everything you need. They have all of the equipment of a normal hospital just like this, only they won't just say you're dying, they will treat you as a challenge. Their goal is to keep you alive, they don't quit when you're almost gone. They live with the philosophy that something can make you better."

"And you're sure that this is a safe and clean environment?" I asked.

"Absolutely. It's a Christian place, and I know that Jodi would love to answer any of your questions about it. She loved her time there. She said it's where she got her life, both physically and spiritually. From all of my research, I would say that I trust it more than even this hospital."

"Really?" I said in disbelief.

Jim nodded. "I really think that you should look into it."

"If I do decide I like it, will you help me convince Mom and Dad? All I want is to not be a financial burden to them, and I don't want them watching me die. I want their last memories of me to be healthy and happy ones. If I could really go to this place and accomplish all of that, then I'm willing to look into it."

"It's all of that and more. I really think you ought to look into it. Not that I think your family thinks of you as a financial burden, but it is a great opportunity. I think I could get you admitted too."

Just then Mom and Dad walked in. Jim told them all about it, and they were even more skeptical than I was. Finally at the end Dad shook his head.

"Absolutely not. I don't want Amy being sent to a home." His voice softened. "I want her here, where we can spend time with her and be with her till the end."

But I wasn't convinced, the more I thought about this, the more I thought it sounded good. I mean I had the opportunity to be able to possibly help them discover something that would help other generations of bone cancer victims, and it wouldn't cost very much, and I could be away. So I made Dad and Mom at least promise to pray about it.

It was either that or waste Dad and Mom's money until I was dead.

Two days went by, and no one mentioned the home to me again. So I decided that I was going to have to bring it up.

"Dad?" I said interrupting his quiet corner. He had turned a corner of my room into his office so that he could prepare his sermons and be with me at the same time. I interrupted him a lot, but he never seemed to mind.

"Yes, Honey?"

"Have you thought about the Ned Home at all?"

Dad sat down his pen and leaned back in his chair. He drummed his fingers against each other and stared at the ceiling.

"I have thought about it. What do you think about it all?" he asked. "I mean you're the one that has cancer, what do you honestly think about it?"

I knew that he didn't like the idea, and that he didn't want to send me away, but he couldn't see it from my perspective.

"Well, Dad, I see it like this. I have the opportunity to go to a place a lot like this, only better, because it is a Christian home, and they might be able to find something to help future generations of bone cancer patients. Just think Dad, if I do this, maybe one of your grandchildren will have a cure when they need it. And it wouldn't be a financial drain on you and Mom. You can't tell me that you aren't struggling. I think it's a great opportunity."

"But you would be away from us. How do you feel about that?" Dad asked.

I paused, I knew that this meant a lot to him. It meant a lot to me too. I bit back my tears and took a deep breath.

"It will be easier for us all if I go now, and we can say good-bye to each other when I'm still healthy enough to appreciate your love. I can call you every day to start with, and Skype you, and as time goes by, I'll call less and less, until I'm gone completely, and it will make the break easier for us all. I know you love me, and I know you're willing, but I don't want you to have to go through watching me die. That's something I couldn't wish upon anyone, especially my own family."

Dad leaned forward. "My dad died of bone cancer, and we had to watch him go through every step, until he was gone. It was hard, I agree, but I don't think I would trade those last few months for anything. When you trust God even in the hard times, His love becomes more real."

"But if I go, there is a chance that my life could affect hundreds. I mean if they can find something that works on me, just think of what that would do for future cancer patients."

"Are you saying that you want to go?" he asked slowly. His brow was furrowed, and his blue eyes looked watery.

"Yes. I want to go. I want to be here with you as well, but you can't imagine how hard it is sitting here, knowing that I'm dying." I choked back my tears. Sniffing a bit I waited till I could begin again. Finally I shook my head. "At least there, I would feel like they were trying to do something. I've prayed about it, and I think that God could use me, if I went, in a way that he could never use me here."

Dad ran his hand through his short blond hair. "Your mom and I have been praying about it too."

"And?" I asked tilting my head forward.

"And we can't think of any reason not to send you besides our own selfish wish to be near you. We've studied this home a lot, and if you really want to go, we'll see."

"Oh I do want to go," I said as enthusiastically as I could. I felt strange begging to go since I was absolutely terrified about it all. But even though I wouldn't tell anyone, I felt a tiny thread of hope. Maybe they would find something to cure me. At least that's what I was praying.

"You would miss Grace's wedding," he said slowly.

"I can watch it over Skype," I said.

"Mom said that if you go, she wants to go and be with you for the whole time, but with Grace's wedding... This is just really bad timing. You would have to go by yourself." Dad sighed. Leaning forward he placed his elbows on his knees and his chin in his hands. "Amy ,this is a huge decision. All of us are going too fast and pray about it for the next two days. I want you to pray about it too."

"Thank you, Dad," I said smiling through my tears. My whole family was going to deny themselves food for two days just to pray for me. "I love you Dad."

"I love you too, Amy," Dad said coming over and gently hugging me.

Those next two days were the longest days of my life. I begged God to make it clear to my family whether I should go or not. But more than that, I asked God to help me give thanks regardless of the outcome.

# CHAPTER 21
# FAREWELL 🚓

Everyone was there. Dad, Mom, all my siblings, even Jim was there. They all stood around my bed, with Dad at the foot.

"We've prayed a lot, and done a lot of research, and we feel that God has some reason for wanting you to go to the Ned Home," he began. "We don't want to send you away, in fact my natural fatherly instincts scream at me to keep you here, but I think that God has other plans for you. We've decided to let you go if you want. The final decision rests with you."

All eyes turned to me, and I looked down.

"I've given a lot of prayer to this, and I've thought of little else." I paused. Was this really what God wanted? I scanned the room, looking for a sign. When my eyes fell on my Bible, I knew what I was supposed to do.

"I also feel that God has a plan for me there. I want to go." I blinked back the tears. "I'll miss Grace's wedding, and I'll really miss Paul singing to me." Paul turned red at my complement, but it was true, I loved listening to him sing. He had such a good baritone voice that it just about sent shivers down my spine.

They all held hands around me and went around and prayed for me. A few times someone broke up and couldn't finish praying. But together, we lifted up our concerns to God.

We were all scared about different things. Mom was scared that they wouldn't look after me with the right motherly care that I needed. Dad was scared to let me out of his sight after everything that had happened, and I was extremely thankful for his concern.

Timothy made it very clear to me that he didn't want me falling in love with any cute doctors and Grace made me promise to call often.

Philip asked me if they would let me eat candy there, and Jim wanted to know if they had memory foam mattresses.

Paul slipped over to me and whispered in my ear so that only he and I could hear.

"I have full confidence in you." His warm breath brushed my cheek. "You just make sure that no one leaves that home without drawing a little closer to God."

His words really struck me, I was supposed to live or should I say, die, in such a manner that everyone who saw me would glorify God. Well that was just what I was going to try to do.

The next two days were filled with my family calling me and asking me if I wanted this item or that item with me there, and I didn't really care on most of them.

One day as I sat watching Dad at his makeshift desk, he glanced up at me and smiled. Reaching into his Bible, he pulled out a bookmarker. Scooting his chair to my bed, he held it up for me to see.

"This," he said softly. "Is something that God has used to remind me time and time again that it's my job to love and protect my family. But ultimately we're all in God's caring hands, not mine."

I looked at the bookmarker, and saw a cross with the words under it, 'I gave you my Son. Can't you give me your life?'

"I love you Dad," I said leaning into his hug. I had gotten so used to the tubes and stuff that I didn't mind moving around with them. And fortunately they had taken some off after the first day.

Dad dashed a hand across his face. "Now," he said huskily. "I'm going to send this bookmarker with you. Every time you see it, remember that although I love you more than life itself, God loves you more than I ever could."

*     *     *

Finally the day came for me to go. I was being air lifted from the hospital to the home in Missouri, I was to be accompanied the entire way by professional medical personnel. So there was no danger in my being moved.

When the time came for good-byes, there wasn't a dry eye.

"I love you, Amy," Mom whispered.

"I love you too," I whispered back. "I'll be waiting for you guys in Heaven," I said to them all. If life continued as expected, this would be the last time we ever saw each other on this earth.

When the last good-bye had been said, Dad prayed aloud for me. When he was done, he leaned over me, and his lips brushed my forehead. "I love you, Amy."

He squeezed my hand and I squeezed his back like my life depended on it. His blond hair and blue eyes would forever be etched in my mind. As I stared at his face, I realized that there were a few grey hairs by each of his temples. I didn't remember seeing them before.

"I'm sorry, Dad," I whispered.

"Sorry about what?" He leaned close.

"About being such a stress on you all. But honestly, I don't regret the past. God knew I would need you."

"You're not a stress, Amy. You're a gift from God, and don't you ever forget that."

I nodded through my tears. "I should go now."

Dad nodded, but didn't let go of my hand. Finally he sighed. "See you soon," he whispered, and he let go.

I was lifted into the helicopter, and the door was shut. Through the window, I caught my last glimpse of my family.

Dad had his arm around Mom, and the boys were all standing there waving. Grace and Jim stood there waving as well. It made me happy to see Jim with the family. He was a good big brother.

Every one of them had tears streaming down their faces, and so did I. In the relatively short time that I had known them, they had been my best friends, my prayer partners, and my family.

I'll never lose that last glimpse of them. It will be forever etched in my brain. It was hard to comprehend never seeing them again. I felt so much closer to death without them, but I was also sort of excited; I was starting a new chapter in my life.

The last time I said good-bye to them, I had thought it was the last time I would ever see them, but it wasn't. So maybe God would bring me back before my death, I didn't know.

Was I ready for this new adventure? I don't know if you can ever be ready for something like that. But lying on my back, being paralyzed and dying made me a lot more prepared for it. If I had been sent to this home when I had still been with Uncle Keith, I don't think I would have handled it very well. That's why I was so thankful that God had brought me to the small town of Rifton, Minnesota, before sending me back down south.

So no, I wasn't ready. I'm never ready for what God sends my way, but I don't have to be. His grace is sufficient from day to day. And I knew that without a doubt He would be with me in every tomorrow that I lived. He had already been there. He wasn't going to be surprised, and He would always be there for me just waiting for me to ask for His help.

I closed my eyes fully expecting to never again see my family, or Minnesota, or any of the people that I loved. Never again would I walk, or run. And never again would I look out over the place where I had nearly drowned, twice.

Never again would I be kidnapped and held as hostage. Never again would I have a gun pointed at me. My most dangerous things to deal with now, were going to be needles.

It's easy to say that I will never again do any of these things, but then who knows. I serve a great God and sometimes He surprises me with things that I never expected. So, I guess I shouldn't really say that I will never again do something. So I will close this chapter of my life by saying that I will never again take life for granted. At least, I hope not.

&OTHE END&

# A NOTE FROM THE AUTHOR

Although parts of it may seem unrealistic, many of the things that happened to Amy were inspired by real events in my life.

I really do live on a farm, and there really is a small river behind our barn, with a small slope going down to the river. We really do have a white farm house, and a big woods with a trail in it that leads down to a bench by the river.

Billy, the man at the livestock auction that Mr. Penner called about the cattle, is a real person that my dad always called whenever he had questions about the auction. And we really have borrowed a truck and trailer from a neighbor. Whenever we need another truck, we really do borrow my grandpa's.

The logging truck that blocked the road actually happened in our town.

The verse that Amy focused on about giving thanks, is something that we can all work on. I've found that when we give thanks for every irritation and problem that comes our way, as well as the good things, it really helps our attitude.

I hope *Never Again* has been a challenge to you in some area of your life. If God has convicted you of something, or you have any thoughts or comments, I would love to hear from you.

Remember that even when things happen that you can't see a purpose for, God always has a reason for every trial He sends.

Maybe you've never thought much about having a personal relationship with Jesus, if reading this has inspired you to seek God in new ways I would love to hear from you with any questions or comments.

## ABOUT THE AUTHOR

Priscilla J. Krahn lives on a farm in northern Minnesota, with her parents and two unmarried siblings. She is the youngest of seven siblings and always loved to read all of her older sibling's books. Her love for reading sparked a passion in her to write. If you were to ask her, Priscilla would say that her two passions are "Writing and evangelism." Her goal is to write books that not only entertain, but also share the gospel. If you have any questions or comments, she would love to hear from you. Her email address is priscillajoykrahn@gmail.com or you can write to her at 59404 County Rd. 12 Warroad, MN, 56763. For additional copies of the book, check out her website at www.priscillajkrahn.com. Also, check out her blog at www.priscillakrahn.blogspot.com for current updates, short stories, deleted scenes and more!

(Excerpt from <u>Never Without Hope</u>, book three, in the "Adventures of Amy" series.)

## CHAPTER 1
# THE NED HOME &

As the chopper touched down at the Medical University in Missouri, my heart sank. This was the place where I was going to die.

The excitement and faith I had felt when I had first gotten into the chopper, had washed away, and were replaced by anxiety.

The building looked huge, and unfriendly. But then, I was only fourteen years old and dying of bone cancer. I didn't want to be stuck in a hospital, but because of my spinal injury, I couldn't be out of medical care. That's why I was going to the Ned Home.

"You must be Amy!" I was greeted warmly by a young man in a medical suit. He looked to be about twenty-five, and he smiled like he was greeting me at a surprise birthday party, and not my death home.

"I'm so glad that you could come," he said grinning. His short sandy hair was curly, and his face had a few freckles sprinkled across it. "Now if you will wait just a little bit, we'll get you into a wheel chair, and you can explore your new home."

"I can't be in a wheelchair," I said firmly from where I lay on my back.

"Of course you can. Why couldn't you?" he asked.

"I have a pinched spinal cord, and I'm paralyzed from my waist down," I replied. "Besides that, I have a broken rib, and a missing rib." I let out my breath in a huff. Hadn't they been told anything about me?

"Nonsense. You can ride in a wheelchair if you want to, it's not like you're dying or something." He turned to a young woman who came up to us pushing a wheelchair. She looked to be about the same age.

Despite all of my protests, they helped me into the wheelchair. Now for a normal person that wouldn't have been a problem, but for me, with a broken rib, a missing rib, and cancer infesting the rest of my ribs, it was extremely painful.

"There, that wasn't so bad was it?" the girl said once I had quit breathing like I was dying. "By the way, I'm Dr. Tabi. I'll be spending a lot of time with you while you're here."

"Dr. Tabi?" I repeated.

"Yeah, like the cat. My real name is Dr. Tabitha Mayfield, but everyone calls me Dr. Tabi."

"Okay." I tried to relax but there was enough pain to keep me tense.

"Don't worry, Amy, we'll have you better in no time. There's nothing wrong with you that a little treatment can't fix," Dr. Tabi said smiling.

I froze, well, I wasn't moving before, but I really froze when she said that.

"I was told that you wouldn't be doing chemo," I said.

"Oh, we won't, that won't help you, and that's no fun anyway. We've got some new things to help you. Now come on, we'll show you around your new home. This is Doctor Anderson," she said gesturing toward the young guy that had first met me at the chopper.

"Just call me Dr. Josh." He held out his hand. "I don't like all those big terms, they sound unfriendly," he said winking. When I didn't reach out to take his hand, he patted me on the shoulder instead. "Sorry about that, I guess it would hurt for you to move your hand like that wouldn't it? Well don't worry, we'll fix that." And with that, he pushed me off for a tour of the wing that they call The Ned Home.

I had no desire to be there, especially with a bunch of optimistic doctors who thought I was getting better. But hey, there wasn't anything I could do about it.

As we rounded a corner we came upon an open office door. There was a voice coming from the office, and it wasn't a pleasant one.

"It's wrong for you to fill these people with hope. There is no hope. They are all dying, and will never get better. It's all just a scam. You'll kill them off one by one, and somehow make money off of them. I'll never come to this dreadful place again!"

As we came up to the office door, a young woman in a medical coat stood yelling at an older gentleman in a medical uniform.

"I quit," the young lady said throwing a paper down on the counter. Then she turned and saw us standing there.

"Hey, Sandy," Dr. Tabi said enthusiastically. "This is Amy. She's here to fill in for Jodi."

Stomping up to me, Sandy stuck her finger in my face. "Get out while you still can. They'll kill you here," she said in a harsh voice that sent chills up and down my spine. With those words, she turned and stalked down the hall.

I looked from Dr. Josh to Dr. Tabi expecting an explanation. They just glanced at each other and Dr. Josh shifted his weight from one foot to the other.

"What have we here?" the elderly man in the medical uniform asked in a soft voice.

"This is Amy, Sir," Dr. Josh said. "Amy, meet Doctor Wilson. He is the head manager here at the Ned Home."

"Well hello, Amy," he said smiling at me. "Please excuse the things you just heard, Sandy was very upset."

I nodded, but I wasn't forgetting what had been said. Was Sandy right? Were they just going to speed up my death here?

"What did Sandy mean by what she said?" I asked.

Doctor Wilson looked from Dr. Josh to Dr. Tabi with a helpless look and then he looked back at me.

"I think it would be best if we didn't discuss it," Dr. Wilson finally said in a very serious tone. "Are you enjoying your tour?" he asked changing the subject. His face kept twitching in a nervous fashion.

I nodded absentmindedly. I couldn't forget the words that I had just heard. What did she mean by them?

"Maybe you should take Amy to her room, so she can see where she'll be staying?" Dr. Wilson said calmly, but I got the feeling that he was trying to get us out of the office. I glanced at the desk, and saw some official looking papers, but as I stared at them, Dr. Wilson reached over and flipped them upside down.

"Of course. We'll see you later, Doctor," Dr. Josh said as he gently pulled me away from the office, through a maze of halls and finally down a brightly lit hallway.

This hall looked way different from the others. There were smiley faces painted on the wall, and a few helium balloons floated near the roof.

When we got near the end of the corridor, we came to a T. There was a big sign above each side. One said *Conquerors* and the other said *Champions*. *Champions* was written in a dark blue, and *Conquerors* was written in a hot pink. We went into the door labeled Conquerors.

Dr. Josh threw open the doors while Dr. Tabi pushed me through.

"Welcome to the place where you conquer your problems," Dr. Josh said enthusiastically. He gave a slight bow and with a flourish of his hand he motioned about the room.

The room was large with five distinct room like areas. They had moveable walls by each one, but they were all pushed back against the wall so it had the appearance of one huge room. I knew without being told which room was mine.

Above the bed's head board, there was a huge picture of Mom and Dad. On the small bed side table there was another picture of my whole family, and the bed was covered in bright blue pillows and blankets. Someone had told them that blue was my favorite color.

At the foot of my bed there was a small dresser, and another young lady was unpacking my things into it. She looked like she was from India.

"This is Dr. Hannah. She's our therapist," Dr. Tabi said pushing me over to her.

"Well hello, Amy. You have the absolutely sweetest family. Look what they sent you," she said holding up a pile of letters.

I started to reach for them, and then stopped in frustration as the pain seared through my side. I couldn't even move my arm without hurting my ribs.

"Don't worry, Amy, we'll read them to you," Dr. Hannah said kindly, but it was just another reminder that I was helpless.

My Bible sat on the bedside table, but I wasn't even strong enough to pick it up. I wanted to snap at everyone but my conscience wouldn't let me. It kept repeating over and over, *In EVERYTHING give thanks.*

"You should meet the other people here in the Conquerors wing," Dr. Tabi said pushing me away from my bed and toward another room like area with a bed in the center of it.

A girl lay on the bed that looked to be in her upper teen years, maybe even twenty. Her hair was snow white, but her eyebrows were a dark, dark brown, almost black.

"Do you dye hair here?" I asked.

"If you want us to we will, but her hair isn't dyed. It changed color because of a head wound. It's rare, but it does happen," Dr. Josh said walking over by the bed. "We call her Lucy," he said. "She has only been here for two weeks, but we're excited to get to work with her."

"What is wrong with her?" I asked as I saw that her eyes were open, but she wasn't responding to the fact that we were there.

"She's suffering from a head wound that was received a few years ago. We're not sure whether she is in the MCS, that means minimally conscious stage, or if she is suffering from something else, but she was in a coma for a long time after her accident. We don't know that much about her. But she comes out of the state that she's in now every once in a while, and in those moments she can talk and respond. We believe she is still trying to come fully out of a coma, and it makes everything very confusing to her. We're working on a theory that if she could start to think about her family, and remember things about what happened, and who she is, that it will help her brain wake up. But we really don't know much about her case yet. We've just been observing her so far."

"So you just observe people here?" I asked. I was beginning to think that Sheriff Jim was crazy for suggesting that I come here.

"For the first little while," Dr. Tabi said. "And then we form a theory, and with that theory, we can try to treat them."

"Like Jodi?" I asked, remembering what Jim had said about his half-sister.

"Yes," Dr. Tabi said. "Like Jodi. She responded very well to our treatment, and now she's doing great."

Dr. Tabi started to push my chair along to another section, and I was introduced to Jasmin. A seven year old orphan girl who was blind due to an accident.

It was encouraging to me to know that she wasn't here because she was dying. Maybe they would find a cure for her, and she could leave, like Jodi did. But there was no hope for me.

My tour was concluded with a quick walk through a library and outside deck for our enjoyment. The whole Champion and Conquerors wing had the feel of an actual home. They had a small kitchen set up for us, a living room, a game room, and everything else you can imagine.

"You still need to meet Champ." Dr. Josh's face broke into a grin.

"Who's Champ?" I asked.

"Champ is our mascot. I'll go get him." Dr. Josh turned and left the room.

"Champ, is the Ned Home's dog," Dr. Hannah explained. "He's a Saint Bernard."

When Dr. Josh returned, I was introduced to Champ. He was huge. His head was level with the head rest of my wheelchair. He was mostly white with some large brown spots here and there. Champ put a paw on my lap in greeting, and I tried to pet him without moving my arm.

"Well, what do you think?" Dr. Hannah asked me when I was back at my bed.

"I think it hurts," I said through gritted teeth as she helped me into bed.

"I'm sorry about that. But what did you think of the Ned Home?"

"I think it's as good a place as any to die." I sighed. If only my family could have come with me. Had I been wrong to think God wanted me to come here?

A look of anger flashed across Dr. Josh's face. Dr. Tabi looked like she pitied me and Dr. Hannah looked bewildered.

"We're not going to kill you, Amy. We're here to help you," Dr. Josh said firmly. He knelt down beside my bed so he was on eye level with me. Champ lay down on the rug next to him.

"Hasn't any one told you guys I have bone cancer? The doctor gave me less than two months to live. I'm dying. I came here in the hopes that you could find out something by studying me that would help you cure other generations of bone cancer victims. I'm not going to leave this place alive. I'm dying," I repeated for emphasis.

"Amy, you can't talk like that. With that attitude you probably will die. You have to believe that you can live," Dr. Josh said even more firmly than before.

"But I can't live," I said.

"That's not what my Bible says. My Bible says that I can do all things through Christ who strengthens me. Do you believe that?" he asked.

"Yes, but…" I began.

"But what? You can live with God's help."

"But what if God doesn't want me to live? I think he's calling me home," I said.

"You're right, Amy," Dr. Tabi said. "God might be calling you home. He might want you to die here, and He may not want you to live long. I believe that God wants us to glorify Him when we're living and when we're dying. But it's a whole lot easier to praise Him when we aren't thinking about dying. So praise God for what the Lord has given you. Thank God that you can breathe and talk on your own. Whenever you're tempted to think about dying, just think about all that God has given you. Try to be thankful in everything," Dr. Tabi said, and the way she said it, felt like a challenge.

"I do thank God for what He has given me. But I still think that I'm dying. And I have trouble thanking God for being able to breathe when every breath feels like somebody is stabbing me," I said.

"There is the problem," Dr. Josh said. "You think that you can die. Do you know what Jesus did for you to pay for your sins so that you can't die?"

"Jesus died on the cross to pay for my sins. I believe that with all my heart, but that doesn't mean that I will live forever," I said.

"Yes, it does. Oh, you might die tomorrow. But you won't really be dead. When you are buried here on earth, you will be more alive than you can imagine. If you stay here on earth, you will be living, but if you die and go to Heaven, you will still be living. You can't really die, Amy. The Bible says to 'Fear not them which kill the body but are not able to kill the soul, but rather fear him which is able to destroy both soul and body in Hell.' Do you understand what I'm saying?" Dr. Josh asked me. His steady gaze seemed to be boring holes into my brain.

I slowly nodded. "I think so. It's like that verse that says 'Jesus Christ the same yesterday, today, and forever.' Whether I die or live, Jesus is still God, and He is still taking care of me. So, even if I die, I'll still be living in Him," I said as it hit me.

"You've got it. So, just remember that you serve the God that raised the dead and made the lame walk. True, He may choose to let you die, but He is still just as good and right as if He let you live. So, with that settled, I think I'll leave you ladies to settle in," Dr. Josh said. He stood to his feet and turned to go. Champ stood up and followed Dr. Josh from the room.

I was excited. Dr. Josh was right. I may die physically, but I will always be alive.

"So, what do you think of this place now?" Dr. Hannah asked me.

"I think it's a really awesome home, but I do miss my family." I bit my lip to keep the tears back, then, swallowing hard, I looked up. "What exactly do you guys do here?" I asked.

"Here at the Ned Home," Dr. Tabi said. "You have a group of us college students who have dedicated our medical life to researching and trying to find cures for different things. Dr. Josh's specialty is stem cell replacement, and so he will probably work with you some on that. He believes with the right treatment, he can cure your cancer for good."

Tabi gestured towards Dr. Hannah. "Dr. Hannah, specializes in head and brain things, like Lucy and Jasmin. I specialize in more of an undefined area, you see, I'm experimenting with some different spinal cord complications."

"So do you all work on everyone here, or do you guys have different patients?" I asked.

Dr. Hannah pushed a wisp of her black hair behind her ear. "We all work with each other and help each other, but we all take our little field of expertise, and try to use it to help the patients that need it. I'm sure you've noticed we only have three girls here now, counting you. And we only have two boys here. With fewer patients, each one that is here gets more attention, and personal care. Also, most people don't want to send their kids here. Besides you, no one else here really has any family or choice about being here."

"Is that because they think that you'll kill off your patients?" I asked as I remembered Sandy's words.

Dr. Tabi sighed. "It is true that a rumor has spread around, and we can't really refute it very well,"

I stared at her, "Are you saying that you really do kill your patients?" I asked in shock.

"No, but we had a patient here, who died, and it wasn't a natural death, she died of an overdose of some of her drugs. It seems that someone deliberately gave her too much. We don't know who or why, and so word has gotten out that we murder our patients, but trust me, we would die before we let anyone get in here to harm you," Dr. Tabi said staring off into space. "If we only knew how to stop it," she muttered under her breath.

"You mean there may be a murderer in your midst?" I asked.

"I'm more inclined to think that it was an accident and they were scared to admit it, but it does seem that way. That's why we haven't been taking on many new people lately, because we're worried about this situation. But don't worry about it, just pray," Dr. Tabi said. "God's in control."

Easy for her to tell me not to worry about it. She wasn't the one laying helplessly in a bed with a murderer stalking the hospital…

Made in the USA
Monee, IL
08 November 2021